## ABOUT THIS BOOK

Gaby Kasun, alpha of the Kasun Canyon Pack, is responsible for protecting her people and the magical falls hidden in the mountains in the Wild West. With the threat of war looming, hostile natives, and an emerging new world, she rules with desperate determination, while struggling to ensure her pack's survival.

In the summer of 1820, as the pack prepares for winter, Gaby receives a message of hope from an old acquaintance—promising wealth and security in St. Louis. All she has to do is travel to the big city, collect what the pack needs, and return home before the first snowfall. With no other options available, she and her mate Ric hit the trail, determined to turn things around for their people, no matter the risk.

When Gaby and Ric arrive at the gussied-up, gun-slinging city, they're met with obstacles at every turn. The Creole Elite, a group of tycoons led by Benedicte Trudeau, have other plans for Gaby. The alpha is forced to fight for her life as she battles to save her people and her relationship with Ric.

Supernaturals hidden in plain sight. Concealed love. A life-ending shootout. Gaby must unravel a pack of lies to save herself and her pack.

# LEGENDS OF HAVENWOOD FALLS BOOKS

*Lost in Time* by Tish Thawer

*Dawn of the Witch Hunters* by Morgan Wylie

*Redemption's End* by Eric R. Asher

*Trapped Within a Wish* by Brynn Myers

*Blood and Damnation* by Belinda Boring

*Fated Beginnings* by E.J. Fechenda

*Emeline* by Katie M. John

*Released From a Curse* by Brynn Myers

*A Pack of Lies* by Kallie Ross

*Kiss the Ashes* by Desiree Lafawn

*Hidden Truths* by Colleen Nye

*Wrath and Retribution* by Belinda Boring

*Changing Fate* by Char Webster

*Rise of the Witch Hunters* by Morgan Wylie

*The Drowning Bride* by Seven Jane

Also try the main Havenwood Falls series; the YA line, Havenwood Falls High; the darker, sexier side of town, Havenwood Falls Sin & Silk; and the local supernatural college, Sun & Moon Academy.

Stay up to date at www.HavenwoodFalls.com

## ALSO BY KALLIE ROSS

Defying Gravity: A Havenwood Falls Novella

Written in the Stars: A Havenwood Falls High Novella

Descent: A Lost Tribe (Book 1)

Defend: A Lost Tribe (Book 2)

Evelyn: A Cupid Chronicles Novella

Unbreakable: The Cupid Chronicles

# A PACK OF LIES

## A LEGENDS OF HAVENWOOD FALLS NOVELLA

## KALLIE ROSS

*This story is for Gaby.*
*You are loving, generous, brilliant, and beautiful.*

# PROLOGUE

1860

"*M*omma!" Conall cried from his bedroom.

Ric and I looked at each other, me hoping he would offer to go check on our son. He shrugged. My mate stood in the kitchen over the sink, his hands covered in suds. We had fallen into a routine in the evenings. After tucking Conall into bed, I sat in the living room reading while Ric washed pots and pans.

"We'll have to teach Conall to do the dishes soon," I said with a smile, and tucked a ribbon between the pages of my book to mark where I'd stopped.

"I like that idea, and not only because it means I won't have to do them. My attention would be better spent on you after a long day of keeping the peace," Ric said, his voice low and flirtatious.

He winked at me and chuckled.

After he turned his attention back to his work, I tiptoed over to him and slid my arms around his waist from behind. He had changed clothes when he arrived home after work, but he still had dirt smudged across the back of his neck.

"If a traveler saw you right now, they might mistake you for a miner. It's been a long time since you've worked with a pickaxe, but you get just as dirty as sheriff. You need a bath as badly as that skillet," I teased, nestling my face between his shoulder blades.

"How about you go check on Conall, and I'll fill the tub?" Ric asked.

"Okay, but it's late, and chilly outside," I reasoned, knowing the trough we had in the back of the cabin would be private enough, day or night, but the temperatures grew downright freezing after sunset in the canyon.

Ric turned and held his hands out, so as not to get me wet. "I'm sure I could find a way to stay warm if you'd join me." He growled playfully and leaned down to kiss me.

His lips were full and warm to the touch, and gone again before I could explore them. I tried to pull him closer, but his frame was too wide and too strong. In a blink, he'd turned and started scrubbing the pans again.

My mouth fell open. "Wha—"

Ric interrupted, "You'd better go check on Conall before—"

"Momma?" Conall called innocently. He had gotten out of bed and was standing behind us.

"Oh, cuddle bug, let's get you back in bed." I turned to pick up our solid five-year-old. He was growing up too fast. His round face was becoming more square, like his father's, and his childlike faith was becoming more skeptical. I hated to admit it, but his cynicism had been inherited from me.

"Will you tell me a story?" he asked, with widened eyes and a pouty bottom lip.

I couldn't help myself. "Of course. Which one do you want me to tell you?"

"Don't be too long," Ric said, insinuating more than Conall knew, glancing over his shoulder and smiling at us both.

I giggled, and Conall waved a hand in the air, half delirious from exhaustion. Our boy had been at school most of the day, then ran errands with me in our growing community. Before six years ago, it had only been our wolf pack in the forest surrounding the falls. But in that short time, with the arrival of a party of supernaturals drawn to the magical water, the settlement had tripled in size.

Conall's room was small, but he spent very little time there. He preferred to be outside. His patchwork quilt hung haphazardly off the foot of his bed. When I sat him on his mattress, he laid his head on his pillow and waited for me to spread his blanket over him. He sighed thoughtfully as I sat down at the end of his bed.

"Momma, will you tell me about the time you went to the big city with Daddy?" Conall asked, and a yawn escaped him just before he finished the question.

"Um, sure, but why that story?" I wondered out loud and tucked his covers under his feet. Ric must have told him about our trip to St. Louis, because I had spent the last twenty years trying to forget it.

"Because I wanna go there someday and be just like Daddy. I wanna ride a steamboat, and be a gunfighter, and go to a ball," Conall rambled with a second wind of excitement. "And drink at a saloon, and play poker with cardsharps, and have a shootout, and save you from the bad guys, and—"

"Wait just one second," I told Conall, and held a hand up to keep him quiet until I could get Ric in the room. "Ulrich Kasun. You had better get yourself in here to explain exactly what you've been telling our son about St. Louis." I had intended to sound disparaging, but a chuckle escaped me.

I didn't have to yell, because like me, Ric had enhanced hearing. He heard me use his given name, and I expected him to enter the room with his tail between his legs. Ric and I had been on many adventures over the years, but there were certain things you didn't explain to a child, like shootouts.

"Yes, dear." Ric shuffled into the room with his eyes on the hardwood floors, wiping his hands with a small towel.

I cleared my throat, and he looked up. "What's this you've been telling Conall about our trip to the big city?"

"I merely told him the truth," Ric said, looking at Conall and avoiding eye contact with me.

"The truth, huh?" I asked with a little sass.

Ric shrugged.

"Sounds more like a pack of lies," I accused, and straightened my skirt.

Ric walked around Conall's bed and sat opposite me. "Well, then, I'd love to hear your version."

His challenge was accepted.

"This is what really happened . . ."

# CHAPTER 1

1820

*T*he October sun had set the sky ablaze, bright orange and red at the plateau's horizon. Another dry, unseasonably warm day. I'd felt a tug at my chest, and knew Ric was close. Our connection alerted me to his return and provided an excuse to leave our dusty, loud settlement. The quiet place reminded me of a time when our pack wasn't concerned with progress. I had diligently watched for the scouting party Ric was in to return, hoping they would have new supplies in tow to help us through the winter.

As alpha, I could have assigned anyone to the task, but members of the pack had been bickering for weeks about how to deal with our shortages. Coming up with a plan to replenish our supplies before the first snowfall had been my number one priority. I explained we would have everything we needed. The land would provide. But, because of the drought, some argued we needed more. More food, more cabins, more blankets, more tools to mine for gold—their list went on and on, and I had grown weary trying to convince them to see reason. We had to keep our discovery quiet, or greedy settlers would flood the mountains.

At the top of the ridge, near our people's settlement in the forest, peace and tranquility had embraced me. We'd built half a dozen cabins, scattered safely in the forest, and learned to store supplies in natural caves along the canyon walls. From a distance, no one would have suspected a group of people lived in the area.

I lifted my canteen to my lips, and took a long drink. The sound of the falls in the distance had always reminded me that it would provide us with the water we needed, but I wondered if I could provide the leadership my people needed to carry them through to spring. Our forest was like a protective barricade from the outside world, but from inside, with dangerous amounts of snow and ice, it felt more like we were being held hostage.

Ric's mother, our last alpha, would have known what to do.

I closed my eyes and took a deep breath. The smell of burnt grass still overpowered the scent of new growth pushing up through the ash in spots across the plateau. The drought had ruined our crops, but nearby natives had set fires as a warning around the canyon to keep us away from their camps.

"There is nothing left for us here," Nina had said sharply. I'd heard her approach, and turned to find her wearing a long cotton dress and a frown. I thought she should have looked happier. Nina Novak and her husband, Peter, had convinced the pack to abandon our guise as a native tribe and build a proper settlement. The change in appearance had probably been the reason the Ute felt threatened. Our pack's progress made us look more like the people attacking them from the east.

"That's not for you to decide," I told her with conviction, and folded my arms over my chest.

I may have given in when it came to modern conveniences, but we'd held our ground on guarding the falls, even after the Ute tribe rode through and lit the plateau on fire. The neighboring natives had never attempted to invade our land before, but they were being driven off their lands because of war, and what the British, French, and Spanish called progress.

Nina placed a hand on my shoulder and said, "Adele might have chosen you for Ulrich, but she's gone. No one would blame you if you gave up your role as alpha to someone more qualified." She sounded haughty, and her nose tilted up in the air.

"You're right." I shrugged out of her grip. "*Ric's* mother picked me. But the magic in our blood chose to bring us together as mates. Adele understood and made her decision. You're just jealous because you weren't chosen to be either."

Nina hated my nickname for my husband. As Ric's distant cousin, Nina had been born with Kasun blood, alpha blood, but her tactics reminded me of the life we had left in Croatia over a hundred years ago. The Blood Lake Pack had become savage, and Adele's own brother made an attempt on her life.

Some died to get us to the New World, including Adele, but not before naming me as her successor. Our people had lived as humans, with the ability to shift into wolves, for thousands of years. The magic that ran through our blood also called us to our mates.

"Adele forced her will on us all, but without a daughter, your legacy will die," Nina mumbled bitterly and turned to walk away.

"Even without Adele's decision, Ric and I would have mated. You never had a chance with him, and your selfish motives would have us all dead if you were alpha." I bit the inside of my cheek to stop all of my anger from spilling out. The taste of blood filled my mouth.

Nina had been a thorn in my side since we were children. Her ability to hit a nerve and scurry off without apology reminded me of the vermin that threatened our food stores. The rats ate, gorging themselves, and left disease behind.

The hint of a vibration in the ground caught my attention. I turned and tilted my head, tucking my hair behind my ear to listen.

My wolf's heightened hearing alerted me to the approach of two horses, with riders, and a wolf.

Something was wrong.

There should have been two horses and two wolves returning from the scouting trip. Nina must have noticed, too, because she froze. Her mate, Peter, had been a part of the group with Stephen Horvat, Boris Greg, and Ric. The four men had been best friends growing up, but the journey to the New World had tested their bond. After the fire, the men put all of their differences aside to find a way for us to trade for supplies.

Along the horizon, the silhouettes of two riders and a wolf had become more distinct. One man was draped over a horse's back in front of its rider. In a matter of seconds, I was able to make out Ric, a black wolf running at full speed ahead of the horses, and Boris and Peter in human form on horseback. It was Stephen lying limp over Boris's horse.

"Go!" I shouted over my shoulder at Nina. "Get Maria and the others. Meet us at our cabin."

Nina would want to check on Peter, but my alpha orders had a way of overriding any pack member's personal inclinations. I hated having so much power over the others, and rarely asserted it. Nina flinched. And without question, she nodded and proceeded to shift into her wolf form. Her dress, shredded, fell to the ground as she darted toward our settlement.

THE NEXT FEW hours were spent trying to stop Stephen's bleeding. He'd stepped into a fur trader's trap, and the iron contraption had nearly taken his leg. The men had been scouring the area for possible connections to trade. For several days, no one had appeared along any of the paths occasionally used by travelers.

Then Ric explained who'd shown up the previous night, and why Stephen had been so careless in their rush back.

With a low rumble, my mate's voice carried across the room. "A messenger on horseback appeared to have been riding for his life, probably scared of the natives. We waited in the tree line to follow him, but then he stopped and called out for you, Gabriele." Ric reached out and took my hand.

"He knew my name?" I asked, shaking my head in confusion. There were only a handful of people I'd revealed myself to in the New World, and Ric had always stood by my side when we encountered outsiders. "Did you recognize him?"

"No, I'd never seen the man before, but he clearly inspected the area before calling your name out. Like he'd been told exactly where to go and what to say. We all smelled blood, and knew he had to be injured." Ric looked over my shoulder to Peter and Boris. They nodded in agreement, and went back to tending to Stephen, who'd been placed on our bed. "After a few minutes, the stranger climbed down from his saddle. He was in bad shape, and stumbled to the ground, pulling his saddlebag with him."

I squeezed Ric's hand. "What did you do?"

"We waited for him to pass out. It seemed cruel, but it was the only way to make sure he would not ask questions or follow us." Ric slipped his hand out of mine and ran his fingers through his recently cut hair. "He was no trader, because there was no sign of a wagon or furs. Even though we'd taken measures to look like those traveling west, we had to protect the pack and the falls."

"I understand." I nodded, and placed a hand on Ric's arm. He shook his head slowly, struggling to say whatever it was he needed to tell me.

Peter Novak moved across the room to join us. "It is not your fault, Ulrich." Peter patted him on the back. "He could not be saved."

Ric shrugged out of Peter's grip. "We don't know that, because we waited too long," he gritted out, sounding irritated.

"He'd been attacked on his journey to us. What would we have done if he had lived, Ulrich? Send him back to St. Louis, knowing of our settlement? He would have sent others back to take what's ours," Peter claimed with an air of authority.

Since arriving in the New World, we'd encountered natives, explorers, pioneers, settlers, and once, time-traveling witches. The existence of supernaturals was no secret to a pack of wolf shifters, but protecting our secret was the only way we knew to protect our lives.

"Peter, I appreciate your reasoning, and agree with most of it, but do not be mistaken that we have any claim over these falls. In fact, the oath Ric and I took to protect them puts us in servitude, not ownership," I clarified, speaking across the room so the others would hear as well. I hated how Peter and the other men could manipulate Ric.

The Novak, Horvat, and Greg families had grown up with Ric and me in Croatia. We'd chosen to follow Adele Jezero, our alpha, to the New World when war divided our pack and led to the Ottoman Empire taking over our homeland. Through the years, the other couples had begun having children while I struggled to learn how to lead our pack.

I was still learning.

"Of course," Peter said, with a hint of hesitation, and nodded. "You'll want to read the letter we found in the man's saddlebag."

Peter reached into the chest pocket of his coat and handed it to me. I glanced from Peter to Ric.

Ric shrugged.

"Thank you." I took the worn piece of parchment from him and recognized my name written across the front. The black wax seal had been broken at its edge. "Who's read its contents?" I asked curtly, annoyed that any of them would be so bold as to read their alpha's correspondence.

Ric glanced at Peter, then he looked over at Boris, who looked up from Stephen's limp form. I knew they could all read English, because I had taught them. For the first time, I regretted it. They all knew I could use my power as alpha to force it out of them, but instead I left the question open.

Silence.

I looked down at my feet and gritted my teeth together. The sound of boots shuffling on the hardwood floor let out a loud creak. I looked up to meet Ric's gaze.

"We wanted to protect the pack," Ric answered slowly, unsure of himself. I was convinced the others persuaded him to read the letter.

"Outside," I barked at Ric with anger. "The rest of you—" I exhaled, taking in the room. The four walls suffocated me. Our friends called it an advancement from the tepees we'd found shelter in in the past, but I found the cabin more like a cage.

I pushed past Peter and Boris, then turned to face them. "Make sure we don't lose Stephen."

The brisk cool night invited me with a crescent moon peeking through a canopy of trees. If I were not alpha, I'd have shifted and run through the forest surrounding our settlement. The thought reminded me of a time when I could do whatever I wanted without the responsibility of the pack.

My life in Croatia had been spent watching my parents and older brothers fight in support of Adele, the Blood Lake Pack alpha. She'd trusted her wolf pack, not using her magic to bend others to her will, but some took advantage of her trust. There were pack members who had believed Adele was soft. Our battle, fighting for freedom from those who were willing to expose our abilities in exchange for power, was only one in a war that took all my family. Adele had been quick to invite me, a devastated ten-year-old, into her home. Her husband, Matthias, had become a father figure, and their daughter, Nikola, was a best friend. It was her son, Ulrich, whom I struggled to connect with, and it was not until ten years later, on our journey to find a place in the New World, that I understood why.

Ulrich had always been stubborn and quiet. He consistently fell in line with what his friends wanted to do. I relished the days he kept his distance. He infuriated me whenever he called me black sheep, because he said I was too kind to be a wolf.

Somehow, after a few months of traveling through rough terrain and missing home, I realized he had become my home.

My heart had grown to love him, and the magic running through my blood called to him. As is our custom, Ric took my surname when we married. He revealed that he'd been in love with me since the day his mother introduced us and explained I would be a part of their family. Only, Adele had not known at the time it would be as Ric's wife, and not as his adopted sister.

I paced.

Sensing Ric, I didn't want to be mad at him, but his constant attempts to protect me made me feel weak. He hadn't meant to undermine me, but I wasn't sure if Peter had the same good intentions. Ric leaned one of his broad shoulders against a nearby trunk and crossed his arms over his chest.

"What do you want me to say?" Ric asked, wanting to fix the problem before he even knew what the problem was. "I'm not sorry we read it. Otherwise, we wouldn't have rushed back so quickly."

"*We*," I growled. "*We* is you and me. I am insulted you included Peter, Boris, and Stephen, before I was able to determine if they needed to know my business."

I huffed and turned my back to Ric. Looking at his handsome face would only make me more conflicted, even if he wasn't remorseful. I carefully unfolded the paper in my hands and slowly read the words scribbled on the page.

· · ·

*June 12, 1820*

*Dear Gabriele Kasun,*

*I hope my personal messenger has found you well. He has been ordered to protect my message with his life. Since our last encounter in New Spain, my trade business has brought much fortune. It would never have come to fruition if it were not for your daring rescue.*

*I traveled safely back to Louisiana Territory, now known as Missouri Territory, without any altercations with natives or bandits. My family has settled in a town along the Mississippi River called St. Louis. In fact, delegates have approved a proposed state constitution to establish a state of Missouri in the near future.*

*Your hospitality and generosity have not been forgotten, and it would be my pleasure to host you as my esteemed guests at my estate. My wife, Marie, hopes to show you her appreciation for saving my life in person. Our children are also eager to meet the brave woman who fought off a pack of wolves and mended my injured arm without a hint of a scar. Sometimes I think they don't believe me, so you must visit and prove them wrong.*

*Your beautiful furs and precious metals would be welcome for trade, and are handsomely sought after in our parts. It would be my pleasure to broker for any supplies you may need to endure the coming winter. The name Chouteau has grown more well-known since we last met. So follow the map below, and when you arrive in St. Louis find the nearest trading post and ask for me.*

*I look forward to repaying your kindness,*

*Auguste Chouteau*

I LOOKED up from the thick, creased parchment, and Ric searched my face. My eyes widened at the prospect of providing for our pack, but I knew why Ric was defensive about reading the letter.

"This might be the only way we all survive through the winter," I said, waving the letter in front of Ric.

"*Might*? It is the first week of October," Ric said with raised eyebrows, and took a step closer to me. "You won't have time to get there and back before the first snowfall. The falls must be protected. What if you're kidnapped, or someone discovers your magic? What if you don't return at all? I won't let you go." His jaw flexed, and he propped his hands on his hips, making him look more like one of the walls of the cabin.

I glared at Ric until a man's throat cleared.

"You have no authority over her decision," Peter said.

Peter pushed a tree limb to the side and planted himself next to me. The move was uncharacteristic of Peter. I made a mental note, but took advantage of his support.

"What he said." I folded my arms over my chest and nodded in Peter's direction. "Besides, Chouteau will be close to sixty by now. He will pose no threat."

"Why is he reaching out to you now?" Ric asked with suspicion. "Why wait so long? He must have an ulterior motive."

"I'm sure he does," I agreed, remembering his ability to sweet talk me into helping with his fur trade so many years ago.

Auguste Chouteau had been a young fur trader when we first met, and he had happened into our territory late at night. Out of supplies himself, and desperate for food, he spotted smoke from our fires. A wolf patrolling our borders, Stephen Horvat, attacked him without provocation.

As a wolf pack, we've always been connected, and when in our wolf form, we have the ability to communicate thoughts to each other. Stephen had mentally pushed a call of distress out to the rest of us, and by the time I'd arrived, Chouteau had been in danger of losing his arm.

The irony of Stephen lying on my bed with a similar leg injury was not lost on me.

After ordering the pack to retreat, I approached Chouteau in my human form. In disguise as a native tribal woman, I wore animal skins with my hair tied back in long braids. Chouteau had as much reason to fear me as he had the wolves, but calmly pulled out a bag of gold coins and begged for assistance.

After I had nursed him back to health with medicinal herbs, Chouteau and I agreed to trade furs for supplies. He returned to the region annually for eight years. Eventually, I shared news of our settlement discovering some precious metals—small nuggets of gold, and a rare red gold. I sent him back with some of the metal and he returned with more supplies than we could have needed in two years combined.

After those eight years, I had to cut ties. He'd innocently complimented me. Chouteau remarked on how young I still looked, and I knew any future trade would result in more questions than I could honestly answer.

But thirty years later, we needed supplies for winter, and fast. We had mined more gold over the years, and even discovered another vein of the red gold Chouteau liked so much. I had a feeling it would trade better than furs.

Facing Ric, I mirrored the stern look on his face. I knew what I had to do. My word as alpha would be final. Magic would bind my orders to the pack. I had to make sure my words would also protect them.

Ric suddenly placed a hand on my cheek, stopping me, and whispered, "I'm going with you."

# CHAPTER 2

1820

*a* week later, as we'd sprinted across a prairie in the autumn sun, I second-guessed my decision. I hadn't wasted any time. I'd packed a small bag of provisions and gave orders for the others to protect the falls. Stephen's leg wasn't doing much better when we left, so I added medical supplies to the lengthy list of provisions we needed. According to Chouteau's calculations, I could make the journey to St. Louis in two weeks on horseback. What the fur trader hadn't known was that I could shave two days off that trip if I traveled in wolf form.

I wore a leather parcel strapped to my back. The bag contained a pair of trousers, a shirt, dried buffalo, and a few pounds of gold rocks. Ric wore a matching parcel as he ran beside me.

My mate had insisted he join me, and I didn't bother arguing. In over a century of marriage, Ulrich Kasun was still the most stubborn man I'd known. His heart had been in the right place, but I hated to leave anyone else as acting alpha. Any time in the past when I'd met with a trader, or simply needed to get away to breathe, I'd handed my title and responsibility to him.

Before we left the settlement, I gave Nina Novak my responsibilities. There was a glimmer in her eyes after I made the announcement to the pack, and it reminded me of the power-hungry wolves we left in Croatia. Nina usually let her mate, Peter, do all the talking, but we all knew she had the dominant, more conniving personality. I had been tempted to leave Helena Greg in charge, but Nina would have manipulated Helena to do her bidding anyway. Instead, I gave Helena the responsibility of being my eyes and ears while I was gone. She hadn't liked the idea of snitching on her friend, but I quickly reminded her that if Nina acted as alpha with the pack's best interests in mind, then she wouldn't have anything negative to report.

Ric and I were careful to run through the protection and shade of forests for the first few days, but when we reached the plains, the sun beat down on our backs for three days. It was the first time I'd considered shifting back into human form. In the mountains, my thick, black fur had always brought me warmth, comfort, and disguise. But out in the open, I'd never felt so exposed.

The only guidance Chouteau had given us in his map had been in reference to distances and landmarks. He hadn't described the landscapes.

Over the horizon, I recognized the shape of two trees standing alone in a field. The thought of sitting in the cool shade for a while had made me giddy. I increased my speed, and goaded Ric.

"*I'll race you.*" I pushed the thought to my mate.

Ric increased his pace to keep up with me. "*What's the prize?*" he asked.

"*A foot massage?*" I bargained, and looked over at him. In his wolf form, Ric was larger than me, and while my coat was solid black, his black coat was peppered with silver fur.

He countered, "*A foot massage and a back rub.*"

*"Deal. See you at the tree!"*

I pressed my paws to the hard, dry ground, and propelled myself forward as fast as I could. Ric, with more weight to carry, fell behind. The tall grass tickled as it whipped around my legs, and when I reached the edge of the trees' shade, I felt a nip at my hind leg. The pinch had startled me, and I toppled forward in a clumsy somersault. In addition to being bumped and bruised, I felt the hint of a sting on my backside. Ric sauntered past me and touched his nose to the closest trunk.

*"Cheater!"* I accused, shaking off a layer of dirt and grass.

Ric howled and proceeded to shift into his human form. His laughter rumbled in his tanned chest as he reached full height. "I did not cheat. You merely tripped."

I curled my lip, revealing my canine teeth, and let out a growl. Ric quickly unpacked his leather bag and slipped on his trousers, covering his most vulnerable parts.

"How about we call it a draw, and I'll massage your feet if you rub my back?" Ric bargained with a grin. He had probably planned to get a back rub out of our wager all along.

Only, Ric hadn't counted on me using one of his greatest weaknesses against him.

Me.

I shifted into my human skin, magic swirling around me as my muscles stretched and my joints popped. The transformation didn't hurt like it had the first few times I shifted, but felt more like getting out of bed the morning after having worked a long day. I appeared as naked as Ric had been, but I didn't rush to clothe myself. With Ric's full attention, I smirked at him as I circled the trees.

"Are you telling me you don't wish to give me a back rub?" I placed a finger on his chest and drew small circles over one collar bone to the other while I waited for his answer.

"You know, now that I think about it, I may have—"

The sound of a horse neighing in the distance startled us both. I quickly swept up my bag and pulled out my clothes to dress myself. A few gold nuggets tumbled to the ground, and I picked them up, shoving them back inside the leather pouch. Ric moved to block the traveler from seeing me while buttoning up his shirt. As I tucked my shirt into my trousers, I peeked around Ric's shoulder and sighted a wagon being pulled by two horses. A man with copper-colored hair sat perched on a spring seat, wearing an animal-skin coat with fringe and an old brown hat. I could hear him whistling a happy tune. The barrel of his rifle leaned against him like a tired wife. Behind him, in tow, was a pile of crates and barrels.

"This may be the answer to all of our problems," Ric said with a lilt of excitement. He stepped out from the cover of the tree and flattened his hand over his brows to get a better look. "Do you see that wagon? It's at least half full."

"It may be close to full, but even if it carried what we needed, it's only half of what we would require for the winter," I said calmly, trying to be realistic. "Our pack has grown in number since we arrived from Croatia, and I have just heard that Helena and Boris are expecting another baby in the spring."

Ric turned to face me. The wagon was still at least a mile out. The corners of his mouth lifted, and small wrinkles creased the corners of his blue eyes. I couldn't wait to grow old with Ric, no matter how many more wrinkles appeared over time.

"Do you think we'll be able to share the same kind of news soon?" Ric whispered as he leaned closer. His fingertips brushed over my hips.

The idea of raising children on top of my responsibilities as alpha had been overwhelming. I didn't know how Adele had managed it. The pack was my family, and while I dealt mainly with adults, they didn't always act mature. I felt the pressures of making sure everyone was healthy and provided for, in addition to being a wife. It was difficult to discern whether I had any real friends, other than Ric, because most of the women in our pack "confided" in me with an ulterior motive.

"I think what I've always thought. We'll have children after the settlement actually feels settled," I said with an exasperated sigh, fighting the urge to roll my eyes. "If we constantly have to trade for supplies outside our territory, then there is no guarantee our children will grow up with both parents. I don't want to subject our son or daughter to a life anything like mine. Don't get me wrong —" I rubbed Ric's neck and pulled him closer for a hug. "I loved your family, and I'm grateful they took me in. And I'm thankful to have been raised by my family as long as I was, but being a teenager without my mother and father to help me through my transition was more difficult than I can communicate." I spoke gently.

"I know." Ric wrapped his arms around me and nestled his face in my hair. He didn't argue, because we had already had the argument too many times to count.

Under the trees, standing on flat terrain, over a week's journey from our settlement, I felt at home in Ric's arms. But something, a gut feeling, cautioned me. I didn't know if my unease was over the approaching stranger, the idea of going to a big city, or what we would return to after leaving Nina Novak in charge of the pack.

Ric and I could handle the traveler, or at least outrun him. We had already decided what we would do about Chouteau. The St. Louis fur trader would not only be thirty years older, but he would expect me to have aged. The problem was being a wolf shifter, and living near the magic-filled falls, I had only aged five years at most. I would have to lie and say the Gabriele who saved his life was my mother. As far as the pack, I would have to put them out of my mind until I took care of the first two problems.

"Hey, y'all!" the stranger called, and waved his hat in the air.

Ric lifted his own hand and waved. I lifted the leather straps of my bag over my head and across one shoulder. Glancing at my feet,

I regretted not packing shoes. I had chosen to pack the red gold instead.

"Y'all all right over there?" The man slowed his horses down and yelled out. He pulled his wagon to a stop a prudent distance away from us. I didn't blame him. "Did someone up and rob y'all?"

Ric nodded hesitantly, and I answered, "Yes, if you could offer us some help or direction we would appreciate it."

The man's eyes squinted as he took me and Ric in from head to toe. We didn't carry any weapons, but Ric was an intimidating sight, even barefoot and empty-handed.

"I'm Jacob Martin, but y'all can call me Jake." He nestled his hat back over his head and jumped down to the ground. A cloud of dust bloomed around his boots. "I guess it would be mighty unkind of me to leave y'all on the side of the trail. Especially since whoever held y'all up stole your shoes. That's just downright poor manners, if you ask me, even for a low-life thief," Jake said, sounding exasperated.

He was a head shorter than Ric, closer to my height. He wore a pair of brown trousers secured with suspenders. A pistol hung from his side under a jacket. Jake examined the trees behind us, then turned and rummaged in the back of his wagon for a few seconds. He revealed a small loaf of bread.

Jake moved in my direction, and Ric stepped over to stand between me and the stranger. Jake's eyes widened, obviously threatened.

"I was thinking ladies first, but if you'd rather have the first helping—" Jake said with a shrug.

Ric took the bread and lifted it to his nose. After taking a whiff of the golden brown crust, he handed the loaf over his shoulder to me. I immediately ripped the bread in half, happy to find a fluffy center.

"Thank you," I said to Jake.

Both men mumbled, "Welcome."

They glared at each other for a moment, and I burst into laughter. I shoved an elbow into Ric's side and handed him one half of the loaf as I took a bite of the other.

"Talk about manners," I said around my mouthful. "You will have to excuse my husband. Jake, I'm Gaby, and this is Ric."

Jake tipped his hat, then waved his hand in the air, swatting the matter away like it was a fly, and returned to shifting boxes in his wagon. We didn't need his help, but it was nice to have it. I never could pass up fresh bread. By the chewiness of the loaf's center, I figured the bread had been baked less than a day ago. Chouteau's directions hadn't mentioned a trading post in this area, but maybe Jake knew where we could trade for boots and horses nearby. I would feel better using our gold in a place where there were fewer people to ask questions.

"This is delicious." I smiled at Jake as he turned around with a pair of old boots in his hands. He dangled them out in front of himself, in my direction. "Oh, I couldn't accept those. If you will point us in the direction of the closest town, we'll find help without having to encroach on your supplies."

Jake's nose wrinkled up in confusion. "I'm sure I don't know what encroach means, but I figured you'd wanna wear these so's ya don't step on a roach, or any other critter for that matter."

"Oh," I said in a higher pitch than intended, trying to hold back a giggle. "Why, thank you, again." I nodded and took the boots.

I situated myself on the ground to slip them on. The leather was worn and soft, and the soles were thin. I pulled the laced strings and began tying them together.

"I'm sorry I don't have another pair," Jake said to Ric. "It's a shame someone would go so far as to steal a pretty lady's dress. It's a good thing your man had some extra trousers you could wear, but if you don't mind me sayin', they look mighty odd on a girl." His face scrunched up like he'd smelled something horrible.

I held my hand up in the air, and Ric took it and pulled me up to my feet. "Is there any chance the town where you bought this bread is close?" I asked.

The sun would only be out a couple more hours, and we would need to find water and make camp if the journey was more than a half day's walk. I had a feeling we would need more than horses and boots in the big city. Jake's reaction to me wearing trousers had been frustrating, but if I didn't want to stand out in St. Louis, I would need to buy a skirt.

"That there bread was baked on a farm a day's ride back east." Jake pointed his thumb over his shoulder. "The family and I do business regularly, so I'm not sure they'll take kindly to you two walkin' up without having been introduced or having anything to barter with."

Ric and I traded a glance.

"We only have what you see," Ric said with a tight-lipped smile. "But I'm a hard worker."

"Oh, yeah, well that might be worth somethin' to 'em." Jake nodded. "Where y'all headed anyways?"

"We are meant to meet with Auguste Chouteau in St. Louis," I answered, hoping Jake might recognize the name.

He did.

Jake's eyebrows lifted, and his chin fell. "Well, I'll be! Mr. Chouteau is one of my employers. He'll be horrified to find out about your predicament. You have quite the trip ahead. I wish I could turn around, but I'm on urgent business for one of his partners, Mr. Trudeau." Jake said the name with an air of reverence.

"We couldn't ask you to turn around," I said, and placed a hand on his bicep. "But if you could help us understand what to expect in St. Louis, I would greatly appreciate it."

Jake looked at Ric first, then me.

"Well, then, for starters," Jake said, pointing at Ric, "to make some of the men more amenable to your cause, you might consider introducing yourself as Gaby's brother."

Out of the corner of my eye, I noticed Ric's face contort in anger. His hand opened and closed like he was preparing to punch Jake, so I did the only thing I knew would keep us in his good graces. My hand whipped through the air and connected with Jake's cheek.

~

1860

"Momma, did you really hit him?" Conall looked up at me from his bed with wide eyes and tugged on my sleeve.

The point of telling him a bedtime story was to help him get to sleep, but it was having the opposite effect. Ric scooted closer to me on the bed and chuckled. His knowing blue eyes met mine, and he smiled.

"I did. But I don't want you getting any ideas. It's not all right to go hitting people. Me slapping Jake was only to keep your daddy from hitting him harder. Jake's notion that we'd be better off lying was as unwarranted as the people in St. Louis. But I'm getting ahead of myself," I said with an exasperated sigh.

Conall's head tilted to the side in curiosity. "What's unwarranted mean?"

I pressed my lips together, trying to figure the right words to explain. "When something or someone is unwarranted, it's not right or not reasonable. You know, maybe we should finish this story tomorrow."

Conall's shoulders immediately pulled up to his ears, and the corners of his mouth turned down. "Aw, Momma, please finish the story. I promise I won't ask any more questions."

"Yeah, Momma," Ric said, imitating Conall's whine. "I like the way you're telling it. I'd forgotten about that slap." He raised his eyebrows and grinned, goading me.

"Fine, but you're not going to like the next part," I said and poked Ric in the chest with my pointer finger.

"Why's that?" he asked. Ric rubbed his chest and feigned being hurt. "The next part is when we—"

"Don't go telling my story," I interrupted. Ric's smile let on that he hadn't been trying to annoy me, but was only trying to get me to continue. "Both of you have to button your lips if you want me to tell the true story."

They glanced at each other, then made the motion of securing their mouths shut.

Like father, like son.

I knew it wouldn't last.

# CHAPTER 3

1820

The black horse beneath me galloped at a steady pace. I'd named her Wilhelmina. She liked me better than Ric, and there could have been a number of reasons for that, but she kept positioning herself between us when we stopped to rest. Wilhelmina came across as a protective, nagging grandmother. She wanted her way, and wasn't easily intimidated.

Ric and I had traded riding each day, so I could stretch my legs. Wilhelmina hadn't given us any grief this particular morning, probably because I was in the saddle. We'd been on the trail five days since we'd crossed paths with Jake. Meaning we'd arrive in St. Louis later in the day.

I'd admired the clear skies and light breeze as we kept a steady pace.

Ric, in his wolf form, ran toward me. Wilhelmina's gait stuttered.

*Three men are coming. I don't know how I missed them, but I don't have time to shift and get dressed. They're just over the hill.* Ric's thoughts pressed into my mind.

I pulled on the reins and tucked my heels under Wilhelmina's belly. "You take cover," I said to Ric, pointing to a tree line in the distance. "I'll get past them."

As I steadied my heart rate, I thought back on how far we'd come. We'd left Jake on good terms. His cheek wore a red tint, but it was better than the broken nose I imagined Ric would have left behind. Ric's and my connection as mates made our bond unbreakable, and it wasn't often he came across as a jealous man.

After Jake apologized, and I apologized, we built a fire and hunkered down for the night. He lent us a blanket and cooked up some beans in an old crusty iron pan. He told us stories of St. Louis. I had to pinch Ric three times, because Jake would say something suggestive and I could feel Ric tense up beside me.

Sleep that night had come easy. The next morning, Ric and I decided to leave before Jake woke. I folded his blanket and placed it on the spring seat of his wagon with a small gold nugget. With a little adjusting, I managed to tuck one boot Jake had given me in my leather pouch and the other in Ric's bag.

We shifted into wolves and ran.

It didn't take us a full day to locate the farm Jake had mentioned. We scouted the livestock, barn, and house for at least an hour and decided it would be best if we didn't introduce ourselves. The more people who knew us, the more likely someone could find us or our settlement. So we waited until nightfall to make our move.

Dresses, shirts, trousers, and sheets billowed in the breeze on a clothesline at the side of the house. They looked like a family of ghosts waiting to greet us. Ric and I agreed we would only take what we needed to blend in when we arrived in St. Louis.

We nabbed something for each of us to wear, a horse and saddle from the barn, and a pair of boots from the front porch for Ric. I left a large gold nugget for the family where the boots had been kicked off, hoping it would more than make up for everything we took.

From that night, at least one of us had to stay in human form, dressed in the clothes we'd taken, to ride the horse and carry the rest of our things. The last five days had grown tedious. Ric and I had taken turns riding and running ahead in wolf form to scout, explore, and hunt. We'd been able to avoid every traveling party we might have crossed paths with so far.

I reached the hilltop, and the three men Ric mentioned were a few hundred feet away. Each one was dressed in black and rode his own horse. Their long coats hid any guns they might have carried. My surprise at seeing the men was not because they didn't look like they belonged on the road, but because we should have sensed them long before Ric saw them.

The only explanation was magic.

The closer Wilhelmina sauntered toward the three men, the more sure I was that they were using supernatural power to cloak themselves. At first, I could have sworn the men were brothers, each with fair skin and blue eyes shaded by the rims of their black cattleman's hats. They stopped about fifty feet in front of me, and one of the men tipped his hat in my direction. Getting a closer look, with my heightened wolf vision, I could tell the one who tipped his hat was significantly younger than the other two.

I kept what I believed to be a safe distance between us, and stopped my horse.

"Good morning," the younger man greeted with the hint of an accent. "You're up early." He smiled, and there was something dazzling about him. He was supernaturally beautiful for a man, not unlike Ric, but something more mysterious, a dark magic, shrouded him.

"Good morning, gentlemen," I replied, plastering the most sincere smile I could muster on my face. "Have you ridden from town? St. Louis?"

"We have," one of the older men answered with a gravelly voice, like he'd just woken up. His eyes roved over me, but I also felt magic caress my cheek. "It's no place for a young lady to be riding into without an escort." His ominous tone verged on threatening.

"I have friends I'm meeting, first thing," I said through a clenched jaw.

The man who had remained silent sat up on his saddle a little straighter and said, "You will have to excuse my brother, Leo." He waved a hand out to make the introduction more official. "This is my son, Julius, and I am Andrew Parris."

"It's nice to make your acquaintance," I said with a hesitant nod. "I'm Gabriele."

"Do you wish for an escort into town? We would be happy to oblige," Julius, the younger man, offered with a flirtatious grin.

The grumpiest of the three, Leo, furrowed his brow and frowned at the idea, but did not argue. Andrew chuckled, and looked from his son to me, then back to his son. Julius's mouth twisted in confusion at his father's reaction.

"I believe Miss Gabriele is capable of handling St. Louis without Le Cercle de Lune escorting her," Andrew said and winked at me. "Of course, we wouldn't dare impose on whatever business it is you have in town."

I frowned.

"Wha—" I started, and noticed the three men turn their attention to something past me, in the distance.

I looked over my shoulder, and at the tree line, a black wolf had shown himself.

When I turned back to the three men, they had already nudged their horses forward to ride past me. Leo made a clicking sound with his tongue and passed me first. Andrew moseyed by with a kind nod. But Julius slowed his horse to pause at my side. His knee was less than a foot away from mine.

Julius removed his hat, and his deep blue eyes searched me. "You can never be too careful. There are men in St. Louis who would take advantage of an outsider like you." He looked like his father, but up close I noticed a small scar over his right eyebrow. "Until we meet again," he said with a wink. His hand reached out to stroke Wilhelmina, and he missed, hitting my saddlebag. I heard a clattering sound, but ignored it, thinking the golden nuggets had been shaken loose inside.

Wilhelmina neighed, and I loosened my grip on the reins, allowing her to move on.

WE ARRIVED IN ST. Louis after lunch. Ric and I had noticed the smell of rot and waste before we could see the main street. A tent city stretched a mile downriver from where the more permanent structures stood. We decided it would be best if Ric shifted and we walked into town together. I held Wilhelmina's reins, and she hesitantly followed us through the crowded street.

The sights were as overwhelming as the scents, only in a good way. Buildings stood three stories tall. Steamboats pushed up the Mississippi River like salmon up a stream. And all the people were fascinating to watch. I had never seen so many people in one place. They swarmed like bees at the general store and docks, carrying boxes and baskets. One mention of our being friends of Auguste Chouteau led us to the center of town.

Several wagons and carriages were already traveling in the same direction. We took our time on foot, watching as men and women of means passed us. The passengers of the coaches and open carriages wore their best attire. Ruffles and bright colors stood out from the monotone shades of brown we witnessed coming and going in town. My own faded blue dress seemed to draw attention, but lacked the luster and embellishments worn by the town's higher class.

"This must be it," I said, breathless at the sight of Chouteau's estate. The house—no, mansion—was grandiose and made up an entire block of the city. A wooden porch with carved railings wrapped around the house on the first and second floors. Shutters framed each window. Auguste really had done well for himself. I smiled at the thought of our lost tradesman covered in animal furs wearing a suit instead and posing next to one of the tall white columns at the top of the staircase leading to his front door.

Carriages were lined up in a semicircle at the bottom of the stairs, and a footman guided guests to the porch. As they made their way, the men and women strapped elaborate masks over their faces. They were having a masquerade party.

We'd reached the end of the lane, and Ric took my hand in his and squeezed it. He looked torn, and I knew what he was going to say. So I stopped him with a kiss. Ric quickly pulled away with a frown and turned his head, checking if anyone had seen us.

I wished someone had seen us. It felt like someone kicked me in the chest to see Ric react the way he did.

"You know you can't be doing that," he said, half worried and half apologetic. He took a step back, creating more space between us. "We agreed we would introduce ourselves as siblings, like Jake suggested."

"You mean you decided," I gritted through my teeth. I folded my arms over my chest and lifted my chin. "This is ridiculous. You hated the notion at first, and we don't have time to make friends. We've almost been gone two weeks, and it will take twice that long to get back with supplies in tow. Not to mention, I have a bad feeling about all this." I waved my hands out in front of me at the partygoers.

Ric shook his head. "Your feelings come and go, but Jake made a point I can't ignore," he said softly, and leaned closer, cautious. "You're beautiful. Every man you passed in town made eyes at you, and as your husband, I'm a threat. As a brother, I can be considered an ally."

He nodded to the house. For every one woman in a silk gown, there were ten men in black d'Orsay hats.

"Ugh." I huffed, aggravated. He had a point, but I didn't want to admit it.

I shoved Wilhelmina's reins at him and grabbed the saddlebag. Then I made my way up the grassy lawn to the Chouteaus' front porch. Ric tied Wilhelmina off at a hitching post, then followed me. His posture changed as we marched closer. His squared shoulders hunched forward, and his eyes didn't quite meet mine when I motioned to a line of people making their way around to the back of the house.

"Where could they be going?" I asked.

He shrugged.

The footman greeted me with a smile and a bow, then looked to Ric for an introduction. Having lived my life in a matriarchal society, it was easy to forget that some cultures merely placed a monetary value on women, like they were different breeds of horses. These so-called civilized men made my blood boil, and the intrigue of St. Louis and its progress dwindled.

"Pardon us, I'm Ric Kasun, and this is my sister Gaby Kasun. We're here at the request of Mr. Auguste Chouteau, but it seems we've come at an inconvenient time," Ric said with a congenial ease, and tucked one hand in his jacket pocket.

"If you'll give me a few minutes, I will return with Mr. Chouteau," the footman said to Ric, and his jacket tails floated behind him as he made his way swiftly up the staircase and into the house.

I gritted my teeth, and resolved to find out what was happening behind the house. If the men in St. Louis treated women as an amusement, then I figured I'd best be amusing. Before Ric could stop me, I walked around to the back of the house. Ric glanced from me to the front door, and I knew he wouldn't follow. He had to wait for Mr. Chouteau.

Listening to the rambling guests on the wraparound porch, I overheard a few men discussing steamboat shipments from New Orleans. They mentioned it being the last week of October, and something about celebrating Halloween in style. There were too many guests talking over each other for me to make out any details. I'd slowed as I approached the back of the house, fidgeting with the buckle on my leather bag, and peeked around the corner. Everyone was walking down a marked path through the yard and across the next street, toward the river.

"Why, hello there, darling," a deep voice purred from behind me.

I jumped, and turned to face a broad, tall man with piercing blue eyes and a cigar in hand.

"Hello," I answered, feeling a little startled.

The man tipped his hat and stepped closer to me. He lazily lifted his cigar to his lips. He took a long, sultry drag and exhaled the smoke in small circles above my head. The patience he exhibited while drawing out his introduction contradicted an underlying eagerness I saw in his eyes as he looked me over.

"I'm Benedicte Trudeau, of the Louisiana Trudeaus," he said with a unique accent, and winked. He wore a midnight blue suit, with a matching vest. Like most of the men in attendance, he wore a less ornate mask and had a pistol strapped to his side.

I had no idea who the Trudeau family was, but I recognized his French accent. It reminded me of Auguste's accent when we first met. My face must have looked bewildered. Trudeau dropped his cigar and used the heel of his black boot to put it out.

He held his arm out for me to take.

"You must be new in town. Allow me," he said with a roguish smile, and took my hand, wrapping it around the crook of his arm. As his hand covered mine, the hair on my arm stood up. "So whom do I have the pleasure of escorting this evening?"

# CHAPTER 4

1820

"*H*er name is Gaby Kasun," Ric gritted out as he walked around Mr. Trudeau. "And I'm Ric Kasun, her—"

Ric paused. His eyes darted to meet mine, and his lips flattened into a straight line. My heart held out hope he'd choose to introduce me as his wife.

"Brother," Ric mumbled, like he had to force the word out of his mouth.

Trudeau looked Ric up and down, taking in his brown, worn suit. Ric stood an inch taller than Trudeau, and while Ric's hair was dark and wavy, the hair peeking out from under Trudeau's hat was blonde and straight. The only thing the two men looked to have in common was their muscular build.

A slow smile spread across Trudeau's face like honey. "Why, I must insist that you accompany me this evening to the party." He patted my hand. "And your brother is welcome to join us," Trudeau said nonchalantly to Ric.

I tugged my arm back, but Trudeau held tight. "I'm not dressed for a party, Mr. Trudeau. You'll have to excuse me and my *brother*. We are here to meet with Mr. Chouteau, and then we'll be on our way back home."

"I beg to differ. It doesn't matter what a beautiful woman like yourself is wearing, or not wearing," Trudeau said, sounding slimy, and his smile slid into a deliberate smirk.

The man, if you could call him that, infuriated and disgusted me at the same time. A darkness emanating from Trudeau made me wary of him, similar to the men we'd passed on the road to St. Louis. I decided slapping his clean-shaven face wouldn't change his contemptible behavior, so I had to use his womanizing against him. Ric wouldn't like the idea I'd come up with, but his decision to introduce us as siblings had gotten us into the situation.

"I do appreciate your hospitality," I said coyly and squeezed his arm affectionately. "But we would hate to make Mr. Chouteau unhappy by showing up at his party unwelcome."

"Oh, don't you worry about that, sweet thing. You could never be unwelcome anywhere." Trudeau's reference to me being a thing made my neck burn with anger. "In fact," Trudeau continued, pulling me forward with him into the crowd, "we're all heading to one of my steamboats. There will be dinner, dancing, and I'll introduce you to the Creole Elite."

Trudeau caressed my arm softly, as if he were attempting to coax me forward. His hand left a trail of dark magic I could feel trying to permeate my skin. For some reason I recognized his power, but it couldn't bend my will. I figured if I weren't a wolf shifter, there was no telling what the man could have convinced me to do. In order to keep up Ric's ruse, I went along with Trudeau, and Ric followed close behind.

As we moved with the crowd across the street and toward the

river, Trudeau rambled on about his connections in the city. He intermittently complimented me, and I heard Ric growl once or twice behind us. The people walking with us wore frilly silk ball gowns and formal dark suits. Ric and I resembled brown wilting buds in a field of wildflowers.

The closer we came to the river, the louder the crowd grew. It wasn't until I saw the steamboat we approached that I understood the reason for the commotion. The white water vessel looked more like a floating mansion with giant wheels attached to its back. The boat stood three stories tall. A group of men playing stringed instruments sat on a balcony. A railing around the flat roof protected several couples already dancing.

"You must be hungry," Trudeau said as we approached the ramp propped up between the dock and the first floor of the steamboat.

"I am, but we really must find Mr. Chouteau." I glanced over my shoulder at Ric.

"He'll be joining us as soon as all of his guests arrive, and until then I'll make you—" Trudeau winked at me, and caught me checking on Ric. His mouth turned down. "I mean, the both of you, more comfortable."

"Thank you, but—" I started to pull away, but Trudeau had a supernatural hold on me.

"I insist." His mouth tightened impatiently, and he waved me onto the ramp. "I have a private room on the second floor, and we will get you fed and in a new dress."

Mr. Trudeau's kindness felt overbearing, divisive. He led Ric and me up to his room, and while the narrow staircase made me feel claustrophobic, it led to a spacious room with red carpet and velvet-covered seats. A wardrobe, dressing screen, and chest of drawers, each made of walnut, lined a white wall at the center of the ship, and the other three walls were made up of windows.

The sun was setting over the edge of a grassy hill in the distance, and the sky had turned pink and orange. Lit lanterns hung from decorative iron rods making up the railing on the floor above us. Below us, on the first level of the boat, people mingled and drank from crystal glasses. All of their masks concealed their identities, and a sense of mischief lingered.

Mr. Trudeau opened the door of his polished wardrobe, and a rainbow of colors hung inside. He pulled out an ice-blue gown with cap sleeves and a full skirt, and hung it over the top of the screen. My lips twisted, trying to work out whether it would benefit us or land me indebted to Trudeau if I accepted his gift. Before I could decide, Trudeau retrieved a black jacket and white shirt from the wardrobe and a pair of black pants from the chest of drawers.

"I'll have one of my men bring up a tray of hors d'oeuvres and wait for you on the roof," Trudeau said seductively, taking my hand and kissing it. He looked from me to the dress. "You'll look ravishing in this gown."

He exited the room, pulling the door closed behind him. I hadn't had the chance to refuse. And whatever magic lingered on top of my hand, where he'd kissed me, had been meant to silence me. The scary thing was, I was unsure if it had been my own indecision or the magic that kept me from reacting. As a wolf shifter, our magic had always protected us against other supernatural powers. Our exposure to other supernaturals was limited, though, so I couldn't rule out Trudeau's darkness having an effect on me.

I shook my hand, as if the magic would fall off like water. "I don't like this one bit," I said a little too loudly, angry.

"You can't believe I do either," Ric reasoned, taking a step closer.

I took a step back, bumping into a settee.

"Gaby, please," Ric begged in a soft whisper. "I almost shifted in that staircase, wanting to rip that man's arm off for touching you." He leaned closer and lifted his hand to my neck. He slid his thumb along my jaw, gently guiding me toward him. "I hate this as much as you, but look where it's gotten us. We might meet someone here who can help us trade our gold for supplies."

He smiled enthusiastically, and the moment was gone.

I pushed him aside and disappeared behind the dressing screen. A small table with a bowl, pitcher of water, and towel was hidden discreetly for washing, and I made quick work of removing the grime and sweat from my face, neck, and arms. The dress I'd been wearing was simple, and easy enough to take off by myself. When I pulled the blue silk dress over the screen, I realized I would need help to button up the back. It irked me to have to ask Ric for help. Once I'd fastened as many of the buttons as I could, I bent down to my bag and emptied it of the gold nuggets tucked away. A few red gold nuggets were mixed with the others, and a small black stone rolled out. The rock was polished smooth, and it wasn't any larger than a coin. It looked, and even felt, like a stone I might find along the edge of the falls. Thinking back to the three men I crossed paths with before arriving in St. Louis, I remembered the clattering sound I'd heard when Julius passed me. He must have slipped the stone inside.

I scooped up all of the rocks and stepped out to the middle of the room to find Ric in his suit.

He was incredibly handsome in black. As my eyes drifted from his black hair to his crystal-blue eyes, I thought there couldn't be a better-looking man in St. Louis. Then my eyes reached his trousers. The cuffs of his pants revealed an inch of bare ankle on each leg.

I busted out laughing. After unloading our treasure onto the dresser, I quickly covered my mouth with my hand.

"Maybe we can let out the hem," I suggested between chuckles.

Ric squinted at me, and bent over to tug on one of his pant legs. "I already thought of that. You should have seen them a moment ago."

"Well, then, they'll have to do," I said matter-of-factly, and turned my back to Ric.

There were at least ten silk-covered buttons left to fasten on my dress. I lifted my hair, and looked over my shoulder at Ric expectantly. He quit fidgeting with his trousers and smiled.

"Let me," he said as his fingers grazed one of my shoulder blades.

"That is not *brotherly* behavior," I quipped, and fought a smile because I would remain frustrated with Ric.

"Then it's a good thing I'm not your brother." Ric leaned in and kissed the top of my shoulder.

"Stop it," I said and swatted at him.

*Knock, knock.*

I flinched in a panic, and said, "You are my brother here. Now, hurry."

Ric had a way of making me feel flustered, most of the time in a good way, but pretending to be his sister muddied my feelings.

After Ric tucked each tiny button into its hole, I scooped up the gold and called out for our visitor to come in. Ric took a seat, crossed his legs and got comfortable. A young man entered with a silver tray. He set it down on the top of the dresser and bowed before exiting.

Fruits, cheeses, bread, and two glasses of water were splayed out on the tray. The urge to tuck all the food in a cloth and save it lost out to my growling stomach. I quickly searched the drawers for a small beaded handbag and placed our gold and my rock inside, then tied it around my wrist.

I ate two bunches of grapes and half a loaf of bread. The cheese wasn't like the kind we made at our settlement. It was pungent and had to be cut with a knife, but Ric seemed to enjoy it.

"Are you ready to go find Trudeau?" Ric asked hesitantly.

I nodded, but as we made our way to the door, I grabbed his arm. "You need to know, every time he touches me I feel something."

Ric's jaw tightened.

"Not like that," I said quickly. "There's a darkness about him, and it feels like he's trying to persuade me with magic."

Ric faced me and slipped his hands around my waist. "Why didn't you tell me sooner?" he asked, his bottom lip pouting out, sad I would keep anything from him.

"Because I'm not here for me. I have to think about our pack. You had to know introducing us as siblings would lead to someone flirting with me. It just happens to be this creep, Trudeau. The goal is to find Chouteau and get the supplies we came for. Agreed?"

Ric frowned, regretting his decision, but nodded his agreement.

When we finally made our way to the gathering downstairs, the attendees weren't shy about whispering their thoughts of us to each other. I utilized my heightened hearing to eavesdrop. Some of the women admired my dress, but most of them admired my escort more. When one woman giggled about his pants being too short, my canine teeth pressed against the inside of my top lip. She whispered to her friend that if he wasn't wearing any pants he wouldn't have a problem.

Ric's chest rumbled in a chuckle at the same time, so I knew he'd also picked up on the conversation. At least the women were more discreet about their interest. The men's comments to each other bordered on crude as we made our way up to the roof of the steamboat. I didn't know how Ric stayed calm.

I was still so angry at him, I thought he deserved having to hear it all.

"Well, if it isn't my special guests," Trudeau called from across the rooftop.

The top of the steamboat was surrounded by an iron railing about three feet tall, creating a third story. Men and women appeared to be dressed even more ornately than the people below. Their jackets were embellished with silk to match their partners' dresses, which were decorated with jewels. That's when I noticed Trudeau's jacket lapel had been lined in the same blue silk as my dress. I plastered a convincing smile on my face, and pulled Ric with me over to them.

"It was fate that we met," I said with as much priss as I could muster, and held a hand out to Trudeau. "I cannot tell you how much my brother and I appreciate your kindness."

Trudeau took my hand and kissed it again, but lingered a moment too long. A throb of pain, darkness, crept its way up my arm and down into the pit of my stomach. I fought the urge to pull away and waited for Trudeau to begin the introductions. He was surrounded by a group of men, all older than himself, who looked distinguished and serious. Everyone wore masks except Ric and me, but the accessories didn't hide much. If wrinkles and white hairs measured wisdom, these men would have been the wisest guests at the party.

One of the men's mouths fell open at the sight of me, in awe. I recognized him as Auguste Chouteau immediately, but I couldn't let on that I knew him, since I was supposed to be my daughter. Luckily, Chouteau hadn't seen any of the other pack members in their human forms while he recovered near our settlement. I made sure to protect the others by being the only person he encountered when he returned to trade. If anyone else found out about the prosperity we'd found near the falls, they would try to take it away.

Trudeau pulled me forward, leaving Ric outside the circle of men, and placed my hand in Chouteau's. "This is the man you've been in search of, Auguste Chouteau. Mr. Chouteau, meet Gaby Kasun."

"I cannot believe my eyes," Mr. Chouteau said, stunned. He searched me from head to toe, taking in what must have seemed impossible. I watched as his features scrunched together in question, unbelieving.

"It is a pleasure to meet you, sir," I said warmly, truly happy to see him, and squeezed his hand in mine. "You know my mother, Gabriele. And when we received your letter, we knew we had to visit. She's told us so much about you." I motioned behind me to Ric.

"Is this—" Auguste started to ask and held his hand out to Ric.

"Her brother," Trudeau interjected with a proud smile.

Ric leaned forward and shook Chouteau's hand. "Nice to meet you," he said. Ric's smile was less than genuine.

I shuffled closer to Trudeau to make room for Ric, and Trudeau took advantage of the opportunity, slipping his arm around my waist. With his other hand, he pointed out each of the men surrounding us. Mr. Lane had frizzy brown hair, and was introduced as a doctor. Mr. Clark, the Missouri Territory governor, stood tall and lean, with silver hair. Mr. McNair, a businessman of some sort, had a long face with even longer sideburns growing in parallel to his ears. And Mr. Bates, the secretary of the Missouri Territory, stared at me with dark blue eyes, brown hair falling haphazardly over his forehead. They were all gentlemen, greeting me with a soft squeeze of the hand I offered and shaking Ric's hand firmly.

"You, my dear, have the pleasure of keeping company with some of St. Louis's Creole Elite this evening," Trudeau said and winked at Mr. McNair. "These men, along with a few others, are making Missouri a proper state, and we're building a booming city. It will take dedication and hard work, but with these men on our board of trustees, St. Louis will be the capital of this territory one day." His voice boomed with pride, catching the attention of the men and women mingling around us.

Mr. Clark shook his head, and chuckled humbly. "I'm not sure I can be included in your *elite* group. If it weren't for Auguste here, I wouldn't have had the supplies to explore this magnificent land with Meriwether. God rest his soul." Mr. Clark frowned down at the floor beneath his feet.

Some of the others looked at each other, not sure how to change the subject. Mr. Chouteau pulled out his pocket watch and glanced at the time. Mr. Bates's eyes remained focused on me. And Mr. McNair fidgeted with the fit of his vest under his jacket.

I caught Auguste Chouteau's eye as he looked up from his gold timepiece, and couldn't think of anything to say. Auguste smiled at me the way a father smiled at his daughter, sweet and thoughtful. Trudeau's hand twitched at my waist. Auguste's eyes wandered to the place Trudeau touched me, and his smile melted into a disapproving glower.

"We've actually made the trip here from the West for supplies to take back with us," Ric interjected, startling me out of my thoughts. "Am I right, Mr. Clark, to recall you handling Indian affairs for a time?" he inquired with his eyebrows raised, interested to meet one of the few men on the continent who had the natives' best interests in mind.

I hoped Ric's question would take his mind off the untimely death of his partner, Meriwether Lewis. The rumors of his gunshot wounds being self-inflicted were unkind. It had been years since Mr. Lewis's death, but it was widely known that the two explorers had become the best of friends on their expedition.

"Why, yes," Mr. Clark answered and looked up at Ric expectantly. "Have you encountered natives?"

"Yes, sir," Ric answered with a smile. I could tell he was trying to tone down his enthusiasm.

Mr. Clark stepped to the side, pulling Ric into a conversation. I could feel my mate's eye on me, but knew he'd left me with the others to discuss the reason for our journey. Our pack may have been posing as settlers, but when we first arrived in the New World, it had been easier to blend in as natives. Most of the pack had dark hair, and with time our skin grew tan. While a few of the natives, like the Ute, were violent, most were hospitable. The Cheyenne taught us how to survive off the land. And we did, until some of the pack got it in their heads we needed to jump on the bandwagon of progress.

"Mr. Chouteau, your letter mentioned an opportunity to trade?" I asked, stepping forward out of Trudeau's grasp. "Maybe we can—"

"Now, you don't want to mix business with pleasure," Trudeau lured, moving in to close the distance I'd created.

Mr. Chouteau narrowed his eyes, searching me for a sign. I lifted my hair off my neck and gathered it to drape it over one shoulder, feigning being warm. Auguste Chouteau had been a good trader all those years ago because he could read a person. He took the cue.

"Mr. Trudeau, how about you find Miss Kasun a cool drink and inform the captain we are ready to leave port." Auguste nodded to the staircase leading downstairs and held his arm out to me. "Miss Kasun and I can conduct a little business until you return."

Trudeau's face gave him away for a split second. His smile twitched in annoyance, and if it weren't for my heightened abilities, I might have missed it.

With a sly smirk, Trudeau said, "I shall return soon."

"Not soon enough, I'm sure," I replied, pretending to be a little bashful, and curtsied.

After Trudeau reached the stairs, I shook my head, not believing what had come out of my mouth. Playing the part had come too easily, and it bothered me. I glanced at Ric, and his clenched jaw and balled-up fists let on that it bothered him too.

"Be careful, Miss Kasun," Auguste Chouteau warned in a low voice, and tucked my arm around his. "Getting entangled with Benedicte Trudeau would be like getting caught in that iron trap your mother found me in all those years ago."

## 1860

"Daddy!" Conall exclaimed and sat up in bed. "You never told me you pretended Momma was your sister." He clenched his teeth together and glared at Ric.

"Well, son, I was just taking the advice we'd been given," Ric reasoned.

Conall took my hand in his protectively. "I think you should say sorry," he suggested firmly.

"Believe me, I've been saying sorry for the last forty years," Ric grumbled and shifted on the bed.

"What's that supposed to mean?" I asked, a tad vexed, and turned to face him. My head tilted with burning curiosity at his meaning.

Ric rubbed the stubble along his chin, choosing his words carefully. He watched as Conall relaxed back under his covers and I tucked his quilt around him. I could see Ric's mental wheels turning. He was running his answer through every scenario he could think of to make sure he said the right thing.

"I *am* sorry," he said softly, and with a hint of sadness, he took one of my hands, raised it to his lips, and kissed it. "The only reason I hadn't ever told Conall was because I've been ashamed. And I'll be sorry about it for as long as I live."

I leaned closer to Ric, and he scooted to sit across from me. I laid my head on his shoulder. "I forgive you," I said with a smile and closed my eyes, relishing the moment with my boys.

Ric wrapped his arm around my waist, and I rested against him for a moment.

"Momma," Conall whispered. "Are you gonna finish now?"

# CHAPTER 5

1820

"We have to get out of this godforsaken town," Ric barked at me as he paced in front of my bed.

After the party, the Chouteau family insisted Ric and I stay at their home while we were in St. Louis. We had been escorted up to bedrooms adjacent to each other, and since Ric had introduced us as siblings, no one remarked on my brother being in my room. The mansion had high ceilings, and the front hallway was decorated with tapestries two stories tall. It had been so late when the steamboat arrived back at the docks that we were able to watch the sunrise from the Chouteaus' back porch.

"I have a meeting with Mr. McNair tomorrow," I said in a whisper, and continued to brush my hair with a soft-bristled brush I'd found lying on the dresser. "He'll have an idea of what our gold can buy. He mentioned the closure of the bank last year made the value of gold fall in these parts, but it's on its way back up."

"And what of Benedicte Trudeau?" Ric asked and rolled his eyes.

I turned from my reflection in the mirror and took Ric's hand to stop him. "He invited us to dinner tonight, and I plan to make clear our desire to head home sooner rather than later."

"You watch," Ric growled, pulling his hand out of mine. "He'll find a way to get rid of me, and get you alone."

"Even if he did get me alone, I can take care of myself," I argued and stood to face Ric. "You're the one who wanted to save your own skin and call me your sister. You'll have to deal with the consequences."

"Believe me, I'm dealing," Ric gritted out, brushing past me as he headed for the door.

Ignoring his pouting, I reminded him, "Besides, with Mr. Chouteau's gift of supplies, the pack will have everything they need for winter. I just think we need to know what our gold is worth. Plus, I brought some of the red gold. I want to know more about its value, too."

"Gaby," Ric sighed and leaned his forehead against the door. "I wish you wouldn't show that stuff to anyone. We've got enough trouble with Trudeau drooling all over you."

"He's definitely trouble, but I'll let him down easy," I said, walking over to the door. I placed a hand on Ric's back, and his shoulders relaxed a little. "Maybe you could give me a few tips. If I remember correctly, you had to have a similar talk with Nina before we were married."

Nina Novak never stood a chance with Ric, but that didn't make talking to the obsessive, conniving woman any easier. She'd mated with someone else, but knowing she had feelings for Ric had always made my insides boil. Jealousy was like an iron skillet. When on the fire, it could be useful, but if you tried to handle it without caution, you'd get burned.

"There is a big difference between this situation with Trudeau and what we went through with Nina," Ric said in a low rumble.

"What's that?" I propped both hands on my hips.

"You never had to sit back and watch your mate flirt with another woman. I never gave Nina hope, and Trudeau is basking in it after tonight." Ric didn't look back at me. The muscles at his neck flexed as he twisted the doorknob and exited.

When Ric closed the door behind him, it felt like he sealed off the air from my room. I couldn't breathe. As mad as I was at him, he'd been right about one thing. Benedicte Trudeau had become more than hopeful, almost possessive. And the darkness I felt oozing from him over the guests at the party was proof that he was used to getting what he wanted.

TYPICALLY, I'd never sleep through the day, but after our travels and the party, my body collapsed onto my bed, and I fell into a deep slumber. Dreams of swimming in the cool water of the falls filled my mind. I thought I'd just fallen asleep when there was a knock on my door. Barely any light filtered through the quilt I'd used to cover myself from head to toe.

"Come in," I called out roughly. It felt like my eyelids had been lined with honey, heavy and sticky.

Someone entered my room without a word. I peeked out from under the corner of my blanket and saw a young woman tiptoe to the wardrobe across the room. The chambermaid carried a red silk gown, fancy shoes, and a black cowboy hat with red embellishments. She worked to hang them up quietly. Before she left, she bent over to check the chamber pot at the end of the bed.

Gross.

She hadn't left a message for me, but the dress she'd brought was beautiful. It had puffed sleeves and a broad neckline with black lace trim. The silk had been embroidered with a black floral design at the bottom of the skirt.

After the door closed, I rolled over on my back and stretched. A loud yawn escaped me, and as my limbs curled up, I tucked the quilt back under me. I longed to return to my dream, but realized the sun was no longer high in the sky, but setting outside my window.

I would have to meet Trudeau before long.

I scurried out from under the covers and held the new dress up to my body. I looked in the mirror and admired the sash, knowing it would be flattering on my figure. My hair had tangled up into knots, and would take some time to brush, so I washed up and dressed myself quickly. The shoes were too much, so I opted to wear my old, worn boots. Not everything I wore tonight would belong to Trudeau.

*Knock, knock.*

I opened the drawer I'd stowed our gold in and folded the rocks into the pleats in the sash tied around my waist.

"Come in," I called out, expecting the chambermaid's return to help me get ready.

My dress hung open at the back, where I couldn't reach the buttons. I glanced toward the door, and found Ric looking sheepish. The irony was that with a thought or emotion, he could magically shift into a wolf at any time.

I waved him in and said, "Hurry and shut the door, before someone sees me."

"Sorry," Ric offered softly. When he stepped into the fading light, I noticed the dark circles under his eyes and the stoop of his shoulders.

"Did you not sleep?" I asked, already knowing the answer. I turned my back to him and pointed to the buttons over my shoulder.

He started to fasten them, and whispered, "I've been trying to figure out what to say to you. I'm sorry doesn't seem enough."

Ric's fingers grazed the neckline of my dress as he finished.

"There's no reason to apologize," I said, because I couldn't deal with fixing things and then going off to dinner with Trudeau. "I had a dream we were back at the falls, and it made me wish we were there so I didn't have to go out with that Creole creep tonight."

Ric finished buttoning my dress, and I glanced in the mirror. The connection Ric and I shared could never be severed, not as long as we lived. I could feel how close he stood, and his presence usually brought me peace. But I was still angry at him.

Even if Ric couldn't hold my hand or take me into his arms in public, I knew he would be with me at dinner tonight.

The sound of a horse-drawn carriage clattering up to the front drive of the house disrupted my thoughts of Ric. He jumped, walked over to the window, and reported Trudeau's arrival.

I finished primping and preening while Ric and the Chouteau family entertained our guest. I did my best to pin my hair quickly, and decided to carry my new hat until we stepped outside. Expecting the others to accommodate a man none of them cared for seemed cruel. I had been the one to accept his invitation.

Trudeau's attention had not waned the night before, and because he owned a fleet of steamboats, I knew he had knowledge of the supplies being shipped to and from St. Louis. Benedicte Trudeau was a potential resource I couldn't ignore, even if his intentions weren't transparent.

Ric would have argued he could see right through Trudeau's motives, clearly, but the darkness I felt emanating from him at the party reminded me of a dense morning fog. You can know a path, and might have walked it a hundred times, but fog had a way of disorienting you and making you feel lost.

The saying "Know your enemies" had popped into my mind

when Trudeau invited me to dinner. Only, he wanted to know me in all the wrong ways, keeping me close at his side quite literally. I'd decided I would use the time we spent together, chaperoned by Ric, to get information and be as disagreeable and unpleasant as possible.

As I made my way downstairs, I noticed Auguste Chouteau and Ric in deep conversation at the front door. Trudeau looked up at me from the bottom step. He had leaned against the banister, but as I descended, he snatched up his gold pocket watch and stood straight.

One of the hardwood steps creaked under my foot, and Ric's jaw twitched, but he continued to whisper to Auguste. I'd wanted Ric to be the one looking up at me from the entryway. I had desired to see his eyes sparkling with passion. It was my mate's smile I'd longed to find greeting me.

Instead, I'd found Trudeau with a smug look on his face and his chest puffed up with air. His blond hair had been slicked back, and he wore a light gray suit with red trim that matched the color of my gown.

"Why, I'll be," Trudeau said, his Creole accent thick. "You are a vision."

He held his hand out for me to take, and I did. With a tight smile, I said, "Thank you, sir, you're too kind."

"Benedicte," he said, captivated, and nodded without taking his eyes off me. "I insist you call me by my given name."

He took my hand and turned it over, palm facing up. Bending at the waist, he watched for my reaction as he brushed his lips over my skin. I tried to tug my hand away, but he was too quick. It was as if he'd anticipated how I'd react.

He tsked and shook his head ever so slightly, smirking. "So skittish, yet so alluring. I can't help myself. Your naivete is rare in a city like St. Louis, and oh so enticing."

"Mr. Trudeau," Auguste interrupted with a frown. "I hope you'll take special care of my guests, and be on your best behavior."

Trudeau's smirk morphed into a sneer, then quickly went blank. He clicked his boot heel loudly on the floor as he moved to shake hands with Auguste. The moment their hands connected, Auguste mellowed. A slow smile spread over his face, and he appeared to let go of whatever grievance he bore.

Trudeau had used his power over Auguste. The night before, I'd wondered if he had a dark side and was blackmailing Auguste. But after that display, I was sure it was magic. Trudeau hadn't used one drop of magic on me in the entryway, but I'd had a feeling he tried. His manners, or lack thereof, had gotten under all of our skin in a matter of minutes.

"I plan to show these two the best this town has to offer." Trudeau opened the front door with a flourish and waved Ric outside. I followed, and on the front porch Trudeau took my hand and slipped my arm around his. "Don't wait up!" He hollered over his shoulder with the return of his toothy grin. I had a sick feeling Trudeau thought he *was* the best St. Louis had to offer.

Trudeau's open carriage had been painted red, and was operated by a coachman dressed in black. The driver pulled out a horse whip, and it snapped in the air above two black horses. I placed the cowboy hat on my head, if anything to keep my hair manageable, and it fit like a glove.

Because the Chouteau family lived in the city, it didn't take long for us to arrive at our destination. We'd barely discussed the pleasant weather when the carriage pulled up in front of a brick building with a rowdy crowd gathering out front. The sound of music echoed out of a pair of swinging doors. Loud guffaws of laughter spilled over small glasses filled with amber liquid. Small clouds of white smoke escaped from men's pipes and cigars. A few of the women wore feathers in their hair, but the embellishments paled in comparison to the amount of cleavage most of them showed.

"What kind of place is this?" I asked in shock.

Trudeau stood up and jumped to the ground, laughing. "The kind of place I think you'll like."

My mouth dropped open, and I gasped. Obviously, we'd rolled up to a saloon.

The problem was, no gentleman would bring a respectable woman to a saloon. Either Trudeau had somehow discovered I wasn't always a *woman* or he was up to no good. Ric stepped down from the carriage and winked at me. The gesture was meant to keep me calm. As much as he hadn't wanted me to go out with Trudeau, I caught a glimmer of curiosity in his eyes.

Trudeau reached up and put his hands at my waist to help me down. I flinched, worried he'd feel the gold and the little black stone bunched in my sash. "You said you wanted to talk business, and this is a place of my business."

My feet came down softly on the packed dirt road. I searched the sign above. It read *Saloon* clearly. The few signs I could read along the boardwalk read *Barber*, *Mercantile*, and *Post Office*. Nothing had Trudeau's name on it or mentioned steamboats.

"Do you mean to say you're a bartender or postman?" I asked, confused and still looking for anything with his name. People, dressed in every shade of brown, crossed the street and conducted their business. Some of them stopped to watch us.

"You met me yesterday, but I think you know better." Trudeau straightened his jacket and frowned. "No, I own all of these establishments."

"Good for you," Ric said in a grumble from behind him.

"I'm not sure I understand where you're going with this," I admitted with hesitation. I wasn't sure I wanted to know.

Trudeau rubbed his chin, and one corner of his mouth crept up. "Don't play the fool, Gaby," he said slyly. "I overheard you discussing supplies with Chouteau last night, and then you wanted to meet with McNair about gold prices. I'm in."

I glanced from Ric to Trudeau and felt my eyebrows draw together. "In on what?" I asked.

"The town you're building out west," Trudeau said quietly, as if he had been revealing a secret. He crossed his arms over his chest and leaned back against a post, proud of himself.

"We aren't interested," Ric said flatly, and folded his arms across his chest.

Ric's passive-aggressive behavior would eventually blow our cover if I didn't find a way to keep Trudeau at a platonic distance. Showing off his acquisitions had proved his highest priority was money. I deduced that playing into his desire for more wealth would distract him from flirting with me and making Ric even more indignant.

I placed a hand gently over Trudeau's elbow and said, "Don't mind Ric."

I stepped up on the boardwalk and made to look like I was inspecting Trudeau's barber shop window. He followed close behind, and in the corner of my eye I saw him reach a hand out toward me. Playing hard to get would only tease a man like Trudeau into pursuing me more decidedly. Instead of walking ahead, I allowed him to wrap his arm around my waist.

"Benedicte," I cooed. "Our little settlement isn't much, and the kind of progress we've seen in St. Louis seems as many years away as it is miles. The land is wild and beautiful, and maybe by the time *we*, I mean, *I* have a dozen children, there will be a mercantile. I can't wait to start a family and fill the territory with boys as wild as the terrain and girls as beautiful as the scenery." Grinning up at him, I caught a flicker of reluctance when I said *dozen*.

Trudeau's hand loosened for a moment, then he squeezed me close.

"I wouldn't need beautiful scenery if you stayed in St. Louis," he said flirtatiously, and winked.

He was impossible.

When I glanced back at Ric, he was shaking his head. My attempt to direct his attentions somewhere else had failed, but I wouldn't give up. The direct approach would have to do, and not only to set Trudeau straight, but Ric and I needed to start our journey back to the falls in the next few days. If we waited much longer, the weather could turn on us.

Trudeau must have sensed my uneasiness, but mistook it for concern. He said, "Don't worry, I'd send a man or two along with Ric to help transport your supplies. We could get—"

"Stop right there, Benedicte," I said curtly. Trudeau's face blanched, and I realized how harshly I'd reacted. I softened my tone and continued, "Please don't say another word. We barely know each other, and Ric and I came here for the sole purpose of helping our family. I'm afraid anything more must be ignored."

"What if I can't ignore my feelings?" Trudeau said gruffly.

"You must," I answered and turned my head away. Ric's fists were balled up at his sides. "I have a meeting with Mr. McNair tomorrow, and he promises to give us a fair trade for our gold. He might even trade us for the red gold, and then we'll be making our way back to the mountains."

"Red gold?" Trudeau asked. His demeanor shifted from hurt to curious. He took a step back and slipped his hands into his pockets. His eyes roamed over me, and he asked, "Do you have it with you? I'd like to see it, if I may."

"It's back at the house," Ric interjected.

Pulling his pocket watch out, Trudeau opened it with a press of a button. He glanced at the time and pressed his lips together in a tight smile.

"Well, it looks like I'm running late for my next appointment. Would you mind if we called it a night?" he asked, distracted and blatantly rude.

"No," Ric answered too quickly.

Trudeau started for his carriage, and I looked from him to Ric.

"What Ric means to say is, we'll walk back to the Chouteaus'. You go ahead," I said with a sigh of relief.

Something clicked in Trudeau. He nodded and leapt onto the first carriage step. I'd wanted him to realize I didn't have any intention of staying in St. Louis, and we wouldn't be doing business with him. But that would have been too easy.

"I hope you have a nice evening," he said with a cordial bow. "It has been a pleasure. Until we meet again."

Trudeau moved to his seat and tapped the side of the carriage. The driver whipped the horses into motion, and they merged into the bustling traffic. I didn't wonder if Trudeau would look back at us, so I turned to face Ric. We both understood his farewell was a promise.

# CHAPTER 6

1820

*R*ic held out his arm for me to take, and I did. The busy streets were filled with townspeople, but not one of them rode in a fancy carriage or wore a silk dress. I had almost felt like I could be myself, except for the red dress. It felt like Ric and I could be a couple.

That had been my first mistake.

"How about a sarsaparilla?" Ric nodded to the saloon with a grin.

"Don't tell me you think this is the kind of place I'd like, too?" I asked with a frown.

A man flew out onto the boardwalk, leaving two doors swinging violently behind him. The crowd inside cheered, and an unseen female hollered, "I don't want to see the likes of you in here ever again!"

Everyone hollered in support, then settled into a steady stream of chatter and glasses clinking together. The place smelled musty.

But something about it felt familiar. I'd never traveled to St. Louis or been near a saloon before, but there was an entity inside the swinging doors calling to me.

After the stranger picked himself up off the ground and wiped the dirt from his pants, he gave Ric and me a dirty look and walked past us. I barely heard the low growl that had rumbled in the man's chest. Ric, by instinct, postured himself between me and the stranger, but he'd kept walking.

Turning back to me, Ric said, "You may not like the place, but I know you'll like the company." Ric's eyebrows bounced up and down, and he gave me a lopsided grin.

"You're probably right," I admitted, and pulled him with me to the swinging doors. "There's something distinctly different about this place."

Ric's grin turned into a grimace. I'd hurt his feelings by not flirting back, but I couldn't ignore the desire to see what was inside. From what I'd heard, saloons were full of drunk men and half-dressed women. It didn't sound like a place I could see myself mingling. But what if this place called to me for a reason? It definitely felt familiar, supernatural. The same way the magical falls had always fostered our pack with energy.

Ric reached forward to open the door for me, and I froze. The main room was two stories tall, with three lit chandeliers hanging from the high ceiling. A bar had been strategically placed across from the front doors, and to the left a set of stairs led to a balcony that wrapped the room on three sides. Light yellow striped wallpaper made the space feel bigger. A wooden railing had been decorated with pretty girls in their undergarments, and behind them dark, wooden doors lined the walls. There had to have been ten of each.

"We don't have to go inside," Ric offered, and started to step backward.

"No, I'm simply taking it all in," I said dryly. My mouth felt like I'd eaten cotton. "Someone in here has something supernatural or is supernatural," I whispered.

"I can feel it too, but faintly," Ric said softly.

The room was filled with a sea of brown. Every table was mahogany with matching chairs, almost all of them occupied. The glasses were filled with golden liquid. Many of the men's faces were sun-kissed bronze. And the men's drab hats, shirts, and trousers were dingy and filthy.

"Can I get y'all something, sweetie?" a woman said cheerfully, navigating between two tables from our right. She wore a pair of brown, wide-legged trousers with fringe at the sides, and a brown hat. Her shirt was tailored like a man's, but made out of a floral print in shades of pink.

When my eyes met hers, I knew. She had magic.

There wasn't much power in her, but I had a feeling that wasn't always the case. Her blond wavy hair had been tied with a piece of leather over her shoulder. She held a tray over her head, and it was covered in glasses filled to the brim. Suds sloshed over the sides when a man pushed his chair back without warning. The blonde pivoted and saved the drinks like she had heightened reflexes, but pressed her hand to Ric's chest to brace herself.

"Two sarsaparillas, please," I said, stepping in her direction so she wouldn't miss that we were together.

"Coming right up," she said as she glanced at me. She patted Ric's chest before pushing off toward the bar. "If y'all will follow me, I'll set you up at a table. You mind sharing?"

"A table?" I asked, clarifying she wasn't referring to Ric.

"That's fine," Ric said. "My *wife* and I don't mind sharing, but we'd prefer more quiet company."

"You got it, sweetie," she said, and sat her tray down at the table next to her. The men each grabbed a glass. In a few seconds, she lifted the tray back up, and we followed her to the far back left corner of the room. The shadow of the staircase and balcony had concealed the table and its lone occupant.

His green hat was dusty and tilted downward so we couldn't see his face. An olive green coat with leather trim hung on his broad shoulders, and white shirt cuffs peeked out at his wrists from under his coat sleeves. His hands were tan and muscular, and they made his empty glass look small as he tapped it lightly on the wooden table.

"Have a seat here," the woman said and dropped her tray in a loud smack. The sound startled the man, and he looked up, clearly irritated. "Two sarsaparillas?" she asked.

She snatched the man's glass and set it on her tray.

"Yes, for us," Ric answered and held a chair out for me to sit down. "Sir, can we buy you a drink?" he asked the stranger.

The man looked from the barmaid to Ric and twisted his mustache-covered lips in thought. He nodded consent, and reached for a silver watch tucked in the pocket of his gray vest.

"I'm Della Rucker, if y'all need anything else," the woman introduced herself as she lifted her tray over her head. "And this is Anson, Anson Corey. I'll be right back with those drinks."

"Mr. Corey, I'm Gaby," I greeted, and pointed to my mate. "This is Ric."

Anson tipped his hat and tucked his watch away. "Please, call me Anson," he said, and his mustache, peppered with silver hairs, spread wide. I knew he was smiling. He reached across the table and held his hand out to me.

I leaned forward and felt Anson's power before our palms met. It hadn't only been familiar, but I'd felt an identical power over a hundred years ago, when I met a family of witches stuck in a time loop.

As my hand slipped into Anson's, he squinted at me and tilted his head to the side. The brown hair on his chin bristled, and he said, "You're not from around here." His voice was raspy, and his words were spoken carefully, like they had more than one meaning.

"No, we've traveled from the mountains in the Missouri Territory to trade for supplies before the winter winds come," I'd said matter-of-factly. I'm not sure why I'd been so forthcoming, but Ric's foot nudged mine under the table in concern.

"You wouldn't be needing much if it's just the two of you," Anson said, leading for more information. "I'm in the business of helping folks who come through town and want to go unnoticed."

"I'm afraid we've already been noticed," Ric grumbled and smiled tightly at me. "Gaby is hard to miss, and in the first few hours of our arrival, the Creole Elite were fighting for her attention."

I swatted the back of my hand at Ric's arm. Whatever had gotten into me was making Ric more loose-lipped than our pack's gossip, Helena Greg. Before placing my hand back in my lap, I felt the remnants of magic brush over my fingertips. Anson Corey was some kind of witch.

"Those men run this town, and you'd best be careful not to get caught up with their sort," Anson said with a frown. "Each one of 'em is heartless, and I should know. I used to work for the worst of 'em, Trudeau."

Ric and I glanced at each other nervously. We'd introduced ourselves as husband and wife. If Trudeau found out, I didn't know how he'd respond. He seemed a proud man, and in my experience, pride never sat well with deceit.

"Maybe you could help us," I said, leaning forward and lowering my voice. "If you've done business with Trudeau, you'll know how I should best cut ties with him."

I gritted my teeth, forcing myself to stop talking. For some reason, I had the urge to tell Anson about our red gold and the rest of our pack waiting at the falls for us. Something nudged the back my mind, not a thought or memory, but something magical. It took all of my mental strength not to succumb to the pull I felt. I met Anson's clear blue eyes, and after another mental nudge, his brows and mouth relaxed, and the magic disintegrated.

Anson cleared his throat. He glanced past my shoulder.

"Here are y'all's drinks," Della chimed in cheerfully. "If there's anything else ya need, just call my name." She winked at Anson and handed him a tall glass filled with amber liquid. Della grabbed the other two glasses by their handles together, and they landed on the table with a thud.

"Thank you," I said kindly, and lifted the sarsaparilla to my lips. The liquid was cold in my mouth, and the notes of vanilla and licorice were comforting and warm.

Anson took a long swig of his own drink, and then casually swirled what liquid remained in his glass, waiting. He was patient, and he acted as though he had all the time in the world.

The crowd in the saloon grew louder the later it got. Men rallied around poker players at multiple tables dotted around the room. A group cheered on two men at the bar chugging beer. All the while, Anson acted as if the place, and his present company, were invisible. While we were trying to save a few dozen people, it felt like Anson was contemplating how to save the world.

"I don't know how, but you're hiding who you really are," Anson finally said, his voice clear but his words still elusive. "I don't think I can work with folks I can't trust."

"I know who you really are, but only because I've met someone like you before," I said. "*They* could be trusted."

Anson waved his hand in the air like he was swatting a fly away, and a current of power passed over us. "*I* can be trusted. You folks are the ones working with Trudeau. So why can't I pick up on your power? I felt you withstand mine. Are you a shifter like him?"

I looked around the room, scared someone would overhear us,

but the throng of drinkers and gamblers continued without paying us any attention. I asked, "How are you doing that?"

Anson lifted one corner of his mouth and answered, "My dear, if you know who I really am, you know that staving off prying ears is merely child's play for someone like me. Now, who are you? And how in tarnation did you get involved with Trudeau?"

Ric took my hand protectively, his way of slowing me down. When I'd become alpha, I hadn't realized the importance of taking my time. If someone came to me with a problem, I wanted to fix it as fast as I could. But I was learning that reacting and responding were two different ways to handle a situation.

"Trudeau is trying to get *involved* with Gaby, not the other way around," Ric defended me, and set his jaw.

Anson looked to me and said, "You are a beautiful young woman, but the same way you've shielded certain gifts from me, you must have cloaked yourself from Trudeau. Otherwise, you two wouldn't be sitting here now. You, my dear, would be paraded around town on his arm as a trophy."

Confused, and a little frightened at his claim, I wondered at how I'd been able to pick up on supernatural activity with Trudeau and Anson, but Trudeau hadn't let on that he knew we had power of our own. I'd even picked up on magic being used by others, like the barmaid, in the saloon.

"I think keeping Gaby as a trophy is his intention, whether he finds out we're wolf shifters or not," Ric said to me, concern etched in the lines around his mouth.

Anson's mouth fell open in wonder. "*Wolf* shifters," he repeated. He rubbed at the back of his neck, thinking, then asked, "What kind of talisman are you using to disguise yourselves?"

"Talisman?" I asked a little too loudly, worried someone would hear me, and shrugged in embarrassment. I'd heard the term before, but from natives. "I wouldn't know the first thing about that kind of magic."

"Well, you've got to be carrying something around with you, even if you don't know it's charmed," Anson said with concern, and looked from me to Ric like he was inspecting us. "Yep, you're definitely the one carrying it, darlin'."

I huffed, and asked, "What kind of object are we talking about? Could it be something as simple as a rock?"

Anson rubbed his chin and thought about it. I reached for the polished stone tucked into the sash at my waist and turned it over in my hand. Finally understanding Julius's purpose for placing the rock in my saddlebag, I couldn't help but wonder what he got out of keeping the truth about us being shifters a secret. I swallowed down the realization that I'd probably find out one day.

"Yes, a powerful witch or warlock could use a stone to hold that kind of magic, but it works better when the object is personal," Anson said thoughtfully. And when I held the black stone up, his eyes widened in curiosity. "May I?" he asked, and held out his hand.

Unsure if I could trust Anson, I looked to Ric. He pressed his lips into a straight line, just as distrustful as me. As alpha, it was my responsibility to make the call. So why had Ric decided to introduce us as siblings with Trudeau, but appeared indifferent with Anson? His passivity in one moment contrasted with his control in another lit an angry fire in my belly.

I leaned forward, ready to pass the stone to Anson, but fisted it at the last second. "How can I be confident you won't take this stone and use it against us?" I narrowed my eyes at him, watching for any signs of betrayal.

"Let me answer you with a question. Could you trust the magic wielder, the one who felt like me, the person you met before?" he asked, sure of himself, and crossed his arms over his chest.

"Yes, but what do they have to do with you?" I asked, exasperated.

"Magic is similar to dialects. And if my magic feels like that of a witch you've encountered before, then they most likely are from

Salem, like my ancestors. Our people suffered a great deal during the trials, and I was the only one in my family to escape. I wandered from town to town until I made a home here in St. Louis. I accepted a job working for Trudeau, because I thought he was like me. Over time, I started a family of my own. It wasn't long before I started to understand Trudeau's intention to brainwash the community and build an empire where everyone does everything he demands. Most aren't powerful enough to fight his magic," Anson said ominously, and nodded at me. "I'm sure that talisman helped, but you must be one powerful shifter."

"Alpha," Ric said clearly, with a determined look in his eyes. He looked from me to Anson, and waited. Ric must have been getting the same vibe I had been since we sat down. Anson could be trusted, but I wasn't sure I wanted to tangle him up in the web we'd woven. He'd mentioned a family.

I set the stone on the table and slid it across the wood. Anson quickly scooped it up and held it up to the lantern light. His inspection was made with a frown, and ended with a grunt. He slid it back.

"It's solid spell work, but dark," Anson explained with caution. "Probably why it went undetected by Trudeau. I'd suggest you keep this with you at all times, while you're in town, that is."

Tucking the rock back under my sash, I admitted, "There are more of us, a growing wolf pack, back in the mountains. We just want to trade our gold for supplies, but we're waiting to find out what we can get for it, and if the red gold we have is as valuable as the regular gold. Could you help us negotiate a fair trade?"

My question was met with a smile from Anson. Ric took my hand in his and kissed the top of it, showing his support. Anson leaned forward and propped his elbows on the table. He linked his fingers together and nodded.

"Red gold, you say? Any chance your gold mine has been

exposed to magic?" he asked, and his smile spread into a toothy grin. "If so, I think we can do business."

As Anson reached across the table to shake on it, the saloon doors swung open forcefully, with no regard for the men they pushed to the side. Benedicte Trudeau stepped inside, and his eyes landed on our table.

# CHAPTER 7

1820

*A*ll at once, Anson's fingers twitched in the air, I ripped my hand from Ric's, and across the room, Della swept in front of Trudeau with a flirtatious giggle. Our magical encasement flickered and disappeared. I stood up and walked over to the bar, watching the reflection of the room in the large mirror behind the bottles of alcohol. Della led Trudeau teasingly by his necktie to a poker table.

I noticed Trudeau looking back to where Anson and Ric sat sipping on their drinks. He shook his head and grabbed a shot glass from the table, then swallowed all of its contents. Della ran a finger along Trudeau's jawline, and he smiled. She murmured something in his ear, but the saloon's patrons had grown so loud even my heightened hearing couldn't catch what she said. Whatever it had been, Trudeau sat down, pulled a wad of currency from his jacket pocket, and laid it on the table.

"Can I buy you a drink?" a man asked in a thick Irish accent.

He sat on a wooden stool, and his suit was nice, not Creole-Elite formal, but clean and fashionable. "I'm Gabriel Doyle, and this is Viktor Azimov."

Viktor tipped his hat in my direction from his stool on the opposite side of Gabriel.

My mouth formed a tight smile, and I nodded.

I needed a distraction, so I said, "It's nice to meet you. I'm Gaby."

Gabriel knocked on the dark wooden bartop and held up two fingers. The bartender poured two drinks and slid them to Gabriel's hand. He set a glass in front of me and held his up in the air, waiting for me.

"A chara," he toasted with a grin.

I had no idea what he'd said, and I felt one of my eyebrows raise in response. I pressed my glass down on the bar. I wasn't about to raise it and mislead the man. I'd already given Trudeau, a member of the Creole Elite, the wrong idea. I wasn't about to do the same with an unknown, and possibly drunk, Irishman.

"Friend," Gabriel clarified in a lower voice, a little less enthusiastic, but not put off by my hesitation.

I lifted my glass timidly and repeated, "Friend."

I had tried to sound good-natured, but I think it came across more heavy-hearted. I downed my drink, hoping to hide my worry. The liquid left a trail of fire down my throat. My eyes darted from Gabriel to the mirror, searching for Ric and Trudeau.

"Are you looking for or avoiding someone?" Gabriel asked in a whisper, his brows lowered as he concentrated on the mirror's reflection. "Maybe Viktor and I could help, seeing as we are now friends."

"Oh, thank you very much, but—" I had started, but Gabriel placed his hand over mine, stopping me mid-thought.

"I'm also a friend to Anson and Della." Gabriel winked slyly.

"Oh," I exhaled, relieved.

Gabriel stood up and maneuvered himself to block Trudeau's view. He lowered his voice and said, "I'll escort you to the back hallway, under the stairs, where you can meet your man. Make sure to walk in front of me so we don't elicit any unwanted attention."

I fought the urge to look back, but still managed to catch Viktor shift on his stool to my right.

"What about you?" I asked him. It felt like we were leaving one of our own behind in battle.

Leaving without Ric, Anson, Della, or Viktor felt wrong. The wolf pack always stuck together, and had always strived for peace. From time to time, we were dragged into other tribes' squabbles, but we lived by a code that supported the pack, not the individual.

"I will create a diversion if needed," Viktor answered in a Russian accent, a devious smile tilting his lips. Just before I turned to walk away, I noticed a set of sharp canine teeth peeking over his bottom lip.

I had sensed they were supernatural, but they didn't smell like wolves. The magic I'd felt in the air around Viktor and Gabriel wasn't like Anson or Della either. They were vampires. I'd never met one before, and in a matter of seconds, I'd become friends with two. They hadn't seemed like any of the rumors I'd heard, natural enemies, and that made leaving with Gabriel less tense. I'd sensed there was no reason to distrust them.

"After you," Gabriel whispered and waved a hand out in front of him.

I walked along the staircase, under the shadow it cast, trying to stay unnoticed. A small doorway was disguised by the mahogany paneling. Gabriel reached his arm around me and pulled a lever hidden within the woodwork. The door opened, and I ducked inside. Gabriel didn't follow me, so I didn't get the chance to thank him.

"Hello," I called out in a whisper, squinting to see down the dimly lit hallway. My heightened ability to see in the dark kicked in, and I found myself alone. The low ceiling had me hunched over, and the wood-paneled walls made the space feel closed in, like I was confined inside a box.

It didn't take long before a sliver of light appeared across the floorboards as someone opened the door behind me. My body reacted instinctively, pressing against the wall. My muscles tensed, and I held my breath.

"Gaby," Ric said in a whisper, after the light disappeared. "Anson told me he'd meet us around back in a few minutes."

I stepped into the middle of the small hallway and nodded at Ric, knowing his eyes had had enough time to adjust. As I turned toward the exit, I felt Ric reach for me. His hand grazed my hip before latching onto my wrist and pulling me back to him. He enveloped me in an embrace, wrapping his muscular arms around my shoulders.

"I wanted to rush to you when I realized those men were vampires," he said into my hair as he leaned into me. "If it weren't for Anson's magic holding me in place, I might have attacked them and given us all away to Trudeau."

"Gabriel and Viktor were very helpful," I said, pulling back to face Ric. He'd wanted to protect me, but Ric needed to know our assumptions about vampires weren't accurate. "In any other situation, I think they'd be a handful, but they're friends with Anson. So I trusted them."

Ric searched my face. He slid his hands up to my neck, and his eyes stopped on my mouth. He leaned in, and his forehead pressed against mine. He waited for me. As annoyed as I was, I couldn't withhold my affection any longer.

I pushed up on my toes and gave in to my desire. I kissed him. His lips accepted my attention, then began to beg for more. I could taste the sarsaparilla on his breath. He kissed my bottom lip and left a trail of soft kisses across my jawline as he nestled his face into my hair. Ric's hands slowly traveled down my arms and lingered at my waist, pulling me closer. We fit together. He belonged in my arms, and I belonged in his.

Lost in the moment, triggered by extreme circumstances, I'd been distracted when the secret door leading to the hallway lurched open. It wasn't until the light revealed us that I realized we'd been found out.

~

1860

"Eww," Conall exclaimed, his face contorting as if he'd bitten into a lemon. "Momma! I don't wanna hear a story about kissing!"

"I'm sorry, sweetheart," I said trying to calm him. "But your daddy and I love each other, so sometimes we kiss. Is that enough storytelling for the night?"

Conall frowned as he took in my words. He hadn't wanted the story to end, but maybe I could convince him to let us finish it the next day. He took my hand in his and looked at Ric.

"I want you to love each other, but can you not talk about the kissing?" Conall's eyebrow lifted in question, the same way his father's did. Both too cute to say no to. "Please, tell me it was Trudeau at the door," he said mischievously.

"What?" I asked in a reprimanding tone. "How could you *want* it to be Trudeau? You have to know it would make him mad."

Conall's enthusiasm faded, and he fiddled with the edge of his blanket. "I just figured this is the part when Daddy has a shootout and beats the bad guy."

I looked at Ric, and my brows furrowed. I couldn't believe his nerve. Ric had been telling the story completely wrong. He'd been lying to our boy. I felt my teeth grate together.

Ric slipped his hand over mine, and said, "Conall, I may have stretched the truth a little when I told you the story before."

I squeezed Ric's hand.

"In fact, I might have told you the story the way I wished it would have gone," Ric added uncomfortably.

I squeezed his hand harder.

Ric glanced at me, then tried again, "Conall, I lied."

I released his hand.

"But why would you lie to me Daddy?" Conall asked with round, curious eyes.

Ric rubbed his chin, thinking through his answer, then he said, "You know how you think shootouts are cool?"

Conall nodded.

"Well, I do too. And, honestly, I've never been in one," Ric said, his voice soft and full of remorse. "I've always wanted to be in a faceoff, like your mommy."

Conall's wide eyes moved from Ric to me. I couldn't tell if Conall believed what Ric told him, but he seemed impressed by the idea. As a mother, the last thing I wanted was for my son to think of me as a murderer. I'd never heard Ric tell his version of the story.

"Momma, will you *please* finish telling me the story?" Conall said sweetly. "I want to be just like you when I grow up."

Conall had always wanted to be like his daddy. I'd never considered he'd ever want to be like me. The notion was more intimidating to me than facing off with Trudeau ever had been.

# CHAPTER 8

1820

*B*enedicte Trudeau snarled at us. He barged into the hallway and took Ric by the shirt. Each of us had been startled. Ric and I were frozen in shock at being discovered, and Trudeau was enraged at the realization that we were not brother and sister. Before Ric could find his strength, Trudeau pulled him out into the open.

"Look at what I've found," Trudeau's voice was rough. He pushed Ric away from him, into a table. "This *dog* was taking advantage of a lady."

Most of the men in the room laughed. I recognized Anson and Della, still sitting at the table near the stairs. The vampires were nowhere to be seen, but I felt dark magic centered around Trudeau and growing stronger. I hadn't felt that much power in one place since meeting the Howe family, but their magic felt pure and light. Whether the power came from one source, Trudeau, or if it emanated from more than one supernatural in the room was something I'd have to figure out quickly.

"I say we put this *dog* down," Trudeau spat out loudly.

I shoved a few men to the side and stood between Ric and Trudeau. I declared, "If anyone's going to be put down tonight, it's you."

A few people snickered, but Trudeau glared at the crowd forming, and they fell in line. Ric regained his footing, but still appeared to be shaken. He took my hand, and two things happened. Trudeau's head tilted, confused by something. And Ric's skin rippled as he fought the urge to shift.

"What are you?" Trudeau addressed me with a sneer, looking disgusted.

I recalled the stone tucked into my sash, and realized Trudeau couldn't see or feel that I was a wolf shifter. He clearly knew Ric was a wolf, considering all the dog jokes, but the talisman had protected my identity. I'd wondered if by holding Ric's hand the stone's power guarded him too.

So to test my theory, I let Ric's hand go.

"I am someone you can't control," I answered him with boldness.

Trudeau's face lightened, almost amused, and he looked from me to Ric. His maniacal laugh echoed through the room, and Ric crumpled to the floor. Everyone in the saloon joined Trudeau's laughter, but I noticed a few people, supernaturals, slip out of the room scared, including Anson and Della.

I scrambled to where Ric lay on the floor and kneeled down beside him. I placed a hand on his shoulder, and within the span of a second or two, I noticed him recovering from whatever dark magic Trudeau had used to hurt him.

"I'm not sure how you're doing it," Trudeau said gruffly, not much louder than a whisper, and his eyes shifted to Ric. "There's more than one way to rid this town of a backwoods liar like you."

Trudeau tucked the front of his jacket behind his sidearm and hooked his thumb in a belt loop. The gesture was relaxed, but he meant it as a threat. He may not be able to use his power to hurt Ric while in my reach, but I couldn't stop a bullet.

"Trudeau, you can put that away," I warned with a scowl. "We'll get out of St. Louis. We'll leave."

I turned and helped Ric to his feet. The movement made a few men flinch around us. They all kept eyes on Trudeau, either out of fear or for permission to act. Some had sidearms, and I sensed more dark paranormal power emanating from others.

"Oh, I expect you both to walk out those doors, but the only way your *brother* will be leaving St. Louis is in a coffin," Trudeau said with an ugly grin and a New Orleans drawl.

"I'd like to see you try to tame the likes of me," Ric provoked. He squared his shoulders and broadened his chest.

Trudeau ignored the attempt at intimidation, and his eyes examined my red dress from its hem to the lace at my shoulders, then moved to the hat I wore. It all belonged to him, and he saw me the same way—a possession.

He looked at Ric, who was smiling defiantly.

"I plan on shooting that smirk right off your face," Trudeau said and nodded to the swinging front doors. "Why don't you meet me outside?"

The crowd around us cheered their consent with awe and a few rowdy hoorahs.

When I looked back at Ric, the eagerness in his wide eyes surprised me. And the determination in his clenched jaw angered me. Then he had the audacity to take a step forward, between Trudeau and me, like he was planning to take the gunslinger on. The only problem was, Trudeau could use his magic to control Ric, making it easier for him to shoot his target.

My hidden talisman would give me an advantage, and the idea of facing off with me might be enough to distract Trudeau. I hated to use my magical influence as alpha to order any of the pack members around, especially Ric, but in this case, it would be the only way to save my mate's life.

"I'll meet you outside, Trudeau," I teased with a wink and nodded behind him.

The room exploded with laughter.

Trudeau chuckled, and when I started for the swinging doors, he waved his hands at the crowd to calm them. After the noise settled into a low hum, he said, "Darlin', you can't be serious. A lady like yourself?"

"I never introduced myself as a lady. You decided to dress me up like one." I picked up my skirt to reveal my boots under the beautiful gown he'd insisted I wear. "Who wants to lend me their gun?" I asked over my shoulder as I stepped onto the boardwalk.

Ric followed behind me, and by the time I'd walked out into the street, a few dozen men and women had filed out of the saloon. I inspected the street and saw Della and Anson in between two buildings, watching the events unfold from a distance. Trudeau flung the saloon doors open, and the bystanders stepped out of the way as if guided by an invisible force. A dark green flicker of magic danced across Trudeau's fingers at his side. I quickly turned to Ric and found him buckling at the waist.

Trudeau was taking his frustration out on Ric.

"Get out of here," I ordered through gritted teeth, and I pushed him in the direction of Della and Anson. "Go! Get the supplies from Chouteau and take them to our family."

Ric cringed.

The words I'd spoken were emphasized with alpha magic. I'd known forcing Ric to leave would hurt him emotionally, not physically. But then he tried to fight against my instructions, and I saw a different kind of pain ripple across his face. A loud cry of agony erupted from him, and I shuddered. There was no way for me to know if it was Trudeau's magic or my own causing him such discomfort.

"Go!" I yelled, and Ric turned and ran.

A thud at my feet startled me. I looked down to find a black leather gun belt. The holster contained a wooden-handled pistol with a silver barrel. I hoped it was loaded, because I'd never handled a gun before. Slowly, I knelt down and picked it up, then buckled the belt around my waist while watching Trudeau stroll to the middle of the dirt road.

"It would seem you need a real man to show you what it means to act like a lady," Trudeau said, and he pulled a cigar out of his coat pocket and tucked it in the corner of his mouth.

The people around us buzzed with curiosity. I, myself, didn't know what Trudeau was up to. He pulled out a match and struck it with a snap of his fingers. After lighting his cigar, he discarded the flame, and pulled out his pistol.

I knew then, he still planned to use his gun.

"Since you're no man and I have no plans to pursue being a lady, how about you tell me the rules to this little game," I challenged and took the pistol out of my holster, turning it over in my hands.

A few people snickered from the sidewalk, but the street grew quiet waiting for Trudeau to reply. He puffed his cigar and carefully released the smoke from his mouth in small circles. He had enjoyed dragging the encounter out. He was as entertained as any of the onlookers.

"The fast draw could be fun, but if you want to stand a chance, a duel would be a better choice," he said, sliding his gun back into its holster.

I mirrored his actions, and secured my sidearm. I created a little more distance between us, sliding back two paces, then asked, "Will you hurry up and decide?"

Some of the people watching shouted out their preference, most eager for the drama of a duel. Trudeau tilted his head up to face the starry night sky, but closed his eyes. His lips tightened and spread thin in deliberation. At first, I figured he'd call the whole thing off. It wasn't until I heard the click of his thumb pulling back the hammer of his pistol that I understood he meant to follow through with his production.

My boots kicked up a small cloud of dirt as I shuffled another step back. My hand shook as it hovered over my sidearm. I grazed my thumb over the hammer and struggled to pull it back. My hesitation hadn't been about the act of killing. I'd defended myself and our pack, and killed men in the process. The difference was that in hand-to-hand combat, I knew I had control. With a gun, the power of the weapon was too easily mistaken for control.

Trudeau had made a similar mistake using his power to control.

His mind made up, Trudeau shook his head madly and met my gaze. His mouth spread into a maniacal smile, and he said, "I don't think I've had this much fun since I left New Orleans. Everyone here is so easy." He flung a hand out and gestured to the crowd. A glittering spray of dark green magic fell over the townspeople, and they were dazzled.

I could feel Trudeau's evil intentions at work, manipulating everyone around him. Even the supernaturals had become pliable under his spell. I quickly surveyed my surroundings, hoping to find an opening. Running might be my only option, but I wouldn't take the chance unless I could find an escape leading away from the direction Ric had left. In the corner of my eye, I recognized Anson now leaning against a post on the opposite side of the street. I couldn't fathom how he'd moved there without me noticing.

"Don't get me wrong," Trudeau said, breaking my train of thought. "Not having others like us vying for position in town has made my plans proceed effortlessly. You would have made an excellent queen in my kingdom."

"That's where you've gotten me all wrong," I said, seeing the real

Trudeau and the lengths he would go to prove himself, and keep his position. I cocked the hammer of my pistol back without wavering. "I'm no queen, nor sidearm for that matter. I'm a leader. And people don't follow me because I force them, but because I wouldn't ask them to go anywhere or do anything I wouldn't do first."

I didn't wait for Trudeau to make the first move, but I tugged the handle of my gun. The barrel slid out of its leather holster, and my finger found its way onto the trigger. I squeezed one eye shut, utilizing my heightened eyesight. I pointed the pistol at Trudeau's chest and pulled the trigger. The shot rang out loudly and was quickly followed by another. I hadn't seen Trudeau retrieve his weapon, but within a moment I felt its blow.

A sharp sting throbbed at the top of my arm. My body jerked, and the black hat I'd worn fell to the dirt.

I reacted before I could think too much about it, and I ran to where I'd last spotted Anson. When I reached the post, the man was gone. I glanced over my shoulder to find Trudeau grinning at me, untouched by the bullet I'd shot at him. He must have used his powers to avoid being hurt. There's no way my aim could have been that off.

"It seems you don't have much of a following anymore," he taunted. "But I promise to find you, and eventually you'll see things my way." Trudeau straightened his jacket and made for his carriage.

"Psst." I heard someone behind me.

Anson stood behind the building in an alleyway. He waved me forward, and I didn't hesitate. Ignoring the pain, I ran as fast and hard as I could. My speed in human form didn't come close to how fast I sprinted as a wolf, but it was still impressive, considering the red gown I wore. It added fifteen pounds. Anson's eyes widened as I approached, and one corner of his mouth turned up.

"Follow me," he whispered.

# CHAPTER 9

1820

*I* woke up on a hardwood floor. A sharp pain shot up into my shoulder from my gunshot wound. It had almost finished healing. I tried to turn toward the warmth an iron stove provided beside me and the muscles in my body spasmed. My hand moved to cover the wound and found it wrapped in a bandage.

"Ugh," I mumbled in a low, dry voice, willing my body to relax.

"Stay still," a female voice ordered sternly from a few feet away. The sound of clanking metal and sloshing water were followed by footsteps. "Here, drink this." Della came into view and knelt beside me.

Her long blond hair fell over her shoulder as she bent down to press a cool tin cup to my lips. She lifted the back of my head with her other hand and smiled when I took a sip. A stubborn wrinkle of worry remained between her eyebrows. I barely knew the woman, and couldn't tell if her concern was for me or herself.

I vaguely remembered following Anson through a maze of back

streets and pathways, and meeting Della at a leaning shack near the river's edge. Her eyes had stared at my arm as I approached. A few feet away from the door, I paused, glanced down at my arm, and collapsed. I'd needed to shift to elicit my shifter magic and heal completely.

There was no way to be sure how long ago I'd passed out. Slender lines of light shone between the boards making up one wall and stretched across the floor. The air around us was crisp and chilly. I'd either woken up with the sun or slept through the day again. I didn't like the idea of either. Losing time meant Trudeau would have had the chance to make good on his promise to seek revenge.

The sound of someone entering the shack caught both Della's and my attention. Della's head snapped up. Her soft features had suddenly turned stony and cold. At the angle I faced, all I could see was brown, wooden walls and a black round stove with a pipe reaching up to the ceiling.

"It's me," Anson said, out of breath. "I found him."

Della released me and stood. Her eyes widened, and I heard someone clamber inside. She asked, "What were you thinking, bringing him here?"

At first, I feared they'd brought Trudeau to finish me off. But I hadn't felt the eerie darkness constantly surrounding him anywhere close. I did, on the other hand, sense something familiar.

My mate.

"Ric?" I asked, and my chest filled with hope. A tear welled up at the corner of my eye, and I bit my bottom lip waiting for his reply.

"I'm here," he said. He rushed to my side and pulled me into his lap. I noticed the gun belt I'd been wearing had been removed, when Ric wrapped his arms around me tightly.

"How?" I asked.

Ric shook his head, taking in the sight of my injury. "I'm not sure," he said solemnly. His eyes were sad and glassy. "One minute I was halfway out of town, unable to refuse your command. And the next minute, your power over me vanished. It was the worst feeling I'd ever experienced, worse than leaving you. It was like you were gone. Dead."

Ric closed his eyes and swallowed down his unease. I couldn't remember what happened after I'd fainted, but it must have been intense. Around us, I could sense Della and Anson moving around the room, avoiding us. The thud of piling items on the table and clank of pans being stacked made it clear they'd busied themselves, but I perceived they were listening in on our conversation.

"Did I die?" I asked loudly, and everyone came to a halt.

"Well," Anson said with some hesitation. "You may have gone a few moments without a heartbeat, but I worked a little of my healing magic. You're lucky it's my specialty." A chuckle lightened his voice as he moved closer to where I lay.

"After a few moments, you were back," Ric explained, sounding relieved. "You were, *are*, in my heart. Your authority as alpha is as strong as ever, but the magic behind the orders you gave me evaporated. They'd been like a wall I couldn't get around, and then I found myself turning and desperately searching for you."

"He was wandering around the Chouteaus' estate when I found him," Anson said sharply. "Foolish, since the whole family's under that voodoo priest's spell. Heck, the whole town's been manipulated by that scoundrel."

"How is it then that we haven't been taken in by him?" I asked, confused, and tried to sit up. Ric wrapped an arm around me and pulled me to lean against his body.

Anson answered, "Well, my magic protects me and my family. After we brought you here, I sent them to make camp with the pioneers along the outskirts of town. We all carry similar talismans to yours." He nodded to me, referring to the stone I had tucked into the fabric gathered at my waist. "Della fell under Trudeau's spell when she first arrived, but—"

"But," Della interrupted, "I came into my own powers recently, and somehow Trudeau can't get inside my head."

"Somehow?" Ric asked with suspicion. His brows furrowed, and he tightened his hold on me protectively.

Della moved across the room and sat on the floor next to us. She was young. Her bright green eyes and flawless skin weren't only perks of being a supernatural—she couldn't have been more than twenty years old. I flexed my own heightened abilities to find something familiar about her, but she didn't smell, look, or sound like anyone I'd ever met before. Her scent was earthy with a hint of floral. It was fresh. She didn't have sharp, elongated canines. And there wasn't a missing heartbeat, or an extra one, for that matter.

"I'm a sylph, a tree faerie," Della explained, and her hard exterior began to fall away. "When I turned eighteen, a few months ago, my supernatural hormones kicked in. See, most people think of fairies as little flying creatures who buzz around the forest. Sylphs are life givers and protectors. When we reach a certain age, we are called to root ourselves. It's kind of like settling down, but instead of building a house or starting a trade, I share my life force with a tree. Once I've chosen, I must unite with that tree every New Moon. I believe Trudeau's magic can't penetrate my mind because I have so much magic inside me. When I share my power with a chosen tree, he may have room to manipulate me. I've fought the urge for some time, but only because I'm afraid of what Trudeau could do to me or make me do. As long as the tree I choose lives, I will live. And the power I'll wield over nature could be used by Trudeau to exploit the river's flow or reshape the city's landscape."

"You're saying you have the power to make the water flow whatever direction you want?" I asked in awe.

"If the water saturates the roots of the tree I join my life force with, then yes." Della's eyes widened, amazed with the idea herself.

"There are forests with trees connected by roots that span hundreds of miles, and my purpose would be to protect them. But being linked to them, I could just as easily destroy them under Trudeau's influence."

Being over a couple hundred years old myself, I'd been under the impression that I'd heard of everything. The only things that surprised me anymore were related to progress, not supernaturals. Della's abilities were like none I'd ever encountered. I was glad she wanted to use her magic for good.

Anson moved to stand behind Della, and said, "Trudeau doesn't know what Della is, and I intend to keep it that way." Anson's fatherly tone was protective, yet gentle.

"Why don't you come with us?" I asked Della, and looked up at Anson for support. "We've settled in a remote canyon, and you could choose any tree in our forest. I have a feeling you'd flourish there, considering our water source."

"I don't want to leave Anson and his family," Della said sadly, and reached up for his hand. "They've helped me so much. If I disappear, I know Trudeau will suspect him."

"Nah—" Anson started, and attempted to wave her worry away.

"Yes, Trudeau would accuse you and use your wife and children against you. You know as well as I do, Trudeau wants power, and if he knew how much we all possessed, we'd be dead," Della said through clenched teeth. "I won't leave without you and your family."

I looked at Ric and realized he'd been watching me. Our connection as mates didn't mean we always agreed, and I could see the concern in Ric's eyes at what he knew I was about to do. My invitation to Della was one more mouth to feed, but Anson's family would be hard to explain to the pack. Especially since we didn't have any supplies to take back with us.

I couldn't, in good conscience, leave any of them behind.

I took a deep breath, mentally pushed through all the doubt that flooded my mind, and said, "You should all come with us."

Ric consented with a tight smile. I could tell he was worried, but I also knew in my heart he supported my decision. I examined Anson's face, and wondered why he hadn't met my proposal with a resounding yes. He twisted his mustache between his thumb and finger instead.

Della's eyes drifted from Anson to Ric and me. With a melancholy voice she said, "Maybe we should all split up. It would create better odds for each of us to escape St. Louis and lessen Trudeau's chances of catching us all."

She had a point.

"He wants me," I admitted, "or at least to figure me out and get his hands on our red gold. We all split up, but I'll set up a distraction and lead him in the opposite direction."

"No," both Ric and Anson said at the same time.

"Why not?" I argued, and pulled away from Ric. The movement sent a sharp pain down my arm, and I froze. "I can't go back to our pack without provisions, and the first snowfall will be soon. Maybe you'll cross paths with that trader, Jake, and he can give you something to take back."

Ric shook his head from side to side stubbornly. Anson's ornery expression, on the other hand, melted into acknowledgement. His mind had been processing all of the possibilities, and he'd come up with a plan.

"We will need to split up," he concurred, "but you won't be the distraction. I will. It's your red gold he wants. Just promise me you'll get my family as far away from Trudeau as you can."

Ric nodded, but something inside me rejected the notion and turned my stomach, like milk turning sour. Anson and I were alike in the sense that we would rather suffer the consequences on behalf of all our family members than have one go through pain. I wouldn't allow him to take on this burden.

"Other than the red gold, what makes you think Trudeau would follow you and not me?" I reasoned with them, hoping we could all agree on something soon. "He's been pursuing me since the moment he laid eyes on me. Until he catches me, I don't think there's anything—"

"Oh, there's something he wants more," Anson said with a grin. "He simply hasn't let on about it. That red gold you carry—it's called copper, and he knows that I can use its power to heal. In the past, I've refused to use my magic for his personal gain, but if he thinks I'll do whatever he wants, he may let the rest of you go."

I'd been so consumed with the building tension between Trudeau and myself that I hadn't considered why Anson consistently avoided the tyrant. I'd been counting on Anson and Della to help us out of St. Louis, but maybe they'd been depending on me, too. If my aim had been truer, and Trudeau's magic weaker, we could have all escaped. As hard as I'd tried, I couldn't think of a way to help them, help ourselves out of town, or solve our pack's dilemma.

Trudeau had each of us right where he wanted us. We couldn't escape this town or him without giving him exactly what he wanted. A low rumble of frustration vibrated in my chest.

I balled up my fist and rammed it into the hardwood floor. I was so mad at myself for not having the answers. The board splintered at my attack, and Ric snatched my hand up to check for an injury. As alpha, I should have been able to come up with solutions.

"Why'd you go and do that?" Ric asked, and he gently kissed my knuckles. "I know I've done my share of idiotic things since we left the settlement, but I think you'll be pleased to know that before Della found me, I collected all of our things from the Chouteau estate, even Wilhelmina, and hid them."

"Where?" I asked, careful not to get my hopes up.

One of the corners of Ric's mouth curved upward playfully, and he admitted, "On that doggone steamboat."

"What in tarnation were you thinkin', son?" Anson exclaimed, and he walloped Ric on the back of the head.

A low growl rumbled in Ric's chest. He barked, "I was thinking it'd be the last place that no-good reprobate would go lookin'."

"He's right," Della said, placing a hand on Anson's shoulder. "Trudeau will be turning this city inside out, but he wouldn't even consider searching his own property."

I leaned into Ric and kissed his cheek. He looked down at me and smiled, proud of himself. As I moved to stand, Ric hopped up and helped me to my feet carefully. We'd been going about everything separately since we left the falls, and the results were disheartening. When we depended on each other and did things together, our circumstances had a way of turning out more favorably. It was then that I realized my mate was my partner and everything in my life would only be better when I included him.

"I have an idea," I said with excitement. "We won't be splitting up, and Trudeau won't be getting his hands on our red gold. In fact, our best chance of us all getting out of St. Louis in one piece will be to stick together. Anson, can you get word to your family and have them meet us at the steamboat?"

# CHAPTER 10

1820

*W*alking across town in broad daylight, without being recognized by one of Trudeau's informants, would have been impossible if it weren't for Anson's magic. Ric and I even considered shifting into our wolf forms, but Anson explained the transformation would have been registered by Trudeau. The only way Anson's magic hadn't been detected was because of talismans he and each of his family members wore, similar to the one I'd been carrying. He told us Trudeau was a voodoo priest, and he had a way of sensing supernatural activity within the city's borders.

We darted from one building to the next. When crossing the street, Anson mumbled enchantments to disguise us. The trek had been less than a mile, but the amount of magic Anson used to conceal us physically, as well as cloak our whereabouts from Trudeau, drained him. Ric had to carry Anson up the stairs when we made it to the steamboat. I concocted an explanation to the ship's crew for being on board, but convinced them Trudeau would be along any minute.

When I joined the others in the sitting room, Ric had placed Anson on the settee. I poured everyone a glass of water to stay busy, while Della kept watch for Anson's family. I raised the water glass to Anson's lips with a shaky hand. If we were going to escape St. Louis, we had to make our move quickly.

Magic had been used to communicate our meeting place with Anson's wife. I'd never met her, and I wondered if she was like Anson—supernatural. With his magic nearly drained, we could use another supernatural's help. But if I was being honest, the amount of power being used made me nervous.

"How are you feeling?" I asked Anson, but I knew his answer. Sweat beaded along his forehead, and his skin had grown pale.

"Weak," he croaked. "My family will be here soon. Please don't leave them."

"We wouldn't," I said and squeezed his hand.

Anson closed his eyes. Before I could panic, he squeezed my hand back.

I looked from Della to Ric and knew the next step in my plan was up to me. Della would work to get Anson's family settled, Ric would watch over Anson and be ready to defend us if anyone realized what we were up to, and I would figure out how to convince the pilot to take us down the Mississippi River. I had a feeling Trudeau would eventually discover we'd taken his boat, but I hoped he'd follow it all the way to New Orleans.

My plan was to abandon ship and travel back to our settlement through the Arkansas Territory. We could stop at Fort Smith for whatever supplies we could scrounge up before traveling through the area inhabited by the Choctaw people. Ric and I were familiar with how to camouflage ourselves among the natives. Once we reached the falls, their magic would protect us, and Trudeau wouldn't stand a chance of finding us.

"I'll need you to signal me when everyone is on board," I said to Ric.

He nodded, and I rushed up the stairs to the pilot house. The crew recognized me from the party, and they were willing to hear me out. But being accompanied by Della and Anson made them wary of my instructions to head south.

The small room perched at the top of the steamboat was made up of windows. We could see in every direction. A large wheel with spokes was mounted at one side for steering, tubes connecting the engine room protruded up through the floor with holes for communicating back and forth, and pedals were rigged to ring the ship's bell and activate the steam whistle.

The pilot paused when, in the distance, we saw a woman and four children running down the dock toward us. Their fast, panicked pace led me to two conclusions. First, someone must have been chasing Anson's family. Second, the pilot wouldn't be agreeing to do anything for me without a little extra enticement.

"I have gold," I said, not bothering with the niceties. "There's enough for you and your men to get out from under Trudeau's thumb and make something of your own."

The man, tall and lanky, looked down at me and narrowed his beady eyes. If he didn't accept my bribe, we'd have to devise a Plan D. There wasn't much time for him to decide or for us to run. Three seconds felt like an eternity.

Thundering footsteps pounded on the stairs, and Ric appeared in the doorway. He looked from me to the pilot, then growled, "We're ready."

I lifted a hand to stop Ric, and the pilot took a step back. Pivoting to turn to the pedals, the pilot pressed one and a loud whistle blew. Ric lunged for him, and I jumped between them. The whistle had been identical to the sharp sound I'd heard at the party before we took off.

And, as I'd predicted, the giant wheel at the back of the boat began to churn. The steamboat lurched forward, and white clouds exited the smokestacks. Before I could sigh with relief, a group of men came into view, all carrying guns. At least ten men filed out from around the Chouteau estate and marched across the street to the river bank. Behind them, I recognized Trudeau yelling orders with hands raised in the air. Sparks of green swirled around him, like a storm.

I could sense his anger.

There was no way to know if his power could reach us, so I ordered the pilot to keep moving. Gunshots were fired, and the sound of shattering glass echoed from below us. We all ducked down and headed for the cover of the staircase. It wasn't long before the men on shore ran out of ammo. Once the fear of being shot again was removed, I noticed the steamboat had stopped moving.

The engines sounded as if they were working at full strength, but to no advantage. I rushed to the top of the stairs and peeked out of a window to find Trudeau's green sparks of dark magic surrounding the boat. The river below us flowed naturally, but the current wasn't carrying us away. We had to do something to keep Trudeau from using his magic.

"Ric, we need to stop him," I said, unnerved.

The problem was, the only thing I'd come into contact with that could block his power was a stone the size of a silver dollar. I rubbed my hand along my sash, and my fingers felt the bump where I'd hidden the smooth black stone. When I'd carried the talisman, Trudeau's magic couldn't take hold. I wondered what would happen to Trudeau if it were to have been on his person or even touched his skin. Would he have been able to project his magic past himself?

I had the craziest notion, and raced to get to Anson and ask what he thought. Ric followed close behind me, and when we reached the sitting room, Anson was surrounded by his family. His wife sat at his side, holding his hand. His daughter had curled up in his lap. And three boys, all the spitting image of Anson, stood around him protectively.

The idea of having so many to love, and love me, warmed my soul. It also ripped my heart out, knowing I was the reason they were in danger.

"Anson, I hate to interrupt, but are you still wearing your gun belt?" I asked from the doorway. I glanced out of the broken windows to the river's edge where Trudeau stood. Della was keeping a close eye on him as well.

Anson nodded, and lifted his daughter to sit in her mother's lap. "You remember what happened the last time you tried to shoot him?"

"I do," I answered, "but I don't think his magic will work on the bullet I'm planning to shoot him with." I fidgeted with the fabric at my waist.

Anson's head tilted to the side.

Della moved from the window to join us, and looked at me knowingly. She said, "It's a brilliant idea, but I think we'll need a shotgun." She left the room and headed down the stairs.

Anson still looked confused, along with his family.

"What are you getting at?" Ric asked from behind me.

I turned to face my mate, and revealed the stone tucked away in the folds of my sash. "This." I held the talisman up in the air.

"Oh," Anson began with realization. "That is brilliant, and it just might work."

"Do you really think it could stop him?" Ric asked, and he reached out to take the stone. He turned it over in his hand carefully, then gave it back to me.

I squeezed it tight, and wished it would destroy Trudeau, but deep down, I knew it would take more to rid him and St. Louis of dark magic. Trudeau's magic was strong and ancient. No matter how many people he had power over, the darkness controlled him. He was merely a vessel.

I admitted, "I think it could give us enough time to get away. And Della's right. We need a shotgun, but we also need the perfect shot."

"I believe I can help with both," Della said as she entered the room with confidence and a rifle propped up over her shoulder.

My chin fell. I gawked at her as she moved to the window and knocked the jagged glass away. Della got down on one knee and braced the stock against her leg while she used the hinge to open the two barrels. I walked over and handed her the stone.

"It's not like a bullet," Anson said. "How are you going to get it to fire?"

"I have an idea for that," Della answered, and pulled a brass shotgun shell out of her pocket. She picked at one end of the cartridge and poured the shots into her hand, then replaced them with the stone. After loading the shotgun, she closed the break, and it clicked. She braced the stock against her shoulder as she took aim.

"What part of him are you planning to hit?" Anson asked, and stood to get a better look outside. Men were running to the dock with belts of ammo.

We didn't have much time before Trudeau's lackeys would reload and start shooting at us again. I didn't care where Della shot him, but the stone needed to make contact if we wanted to limit his power. If she could hit him, embedding the stone inside him, the talisman might block his magic entirely.

"I'm gonna aim for his chest," Della answered. "That way if I'm slightly off, there's a better chance of him still being hit. It won't be lethal, because he can probably heal himself to some extent, but it'll hurt like hell."

Della hunched over and pressed her cheek to the stock. She cocked the hammer and took aim. We were over a hundred yards away.

I inhaled and waited.

The noise around us fell away.

Ric reached over and took my hand.

Della pulled the trigger, and the sound of her shot rang in my ears.

In the distance, Trudeau reached for his upper thigh. The dark magic surrounding the steamboat seemed to dissolve, and I felt the ship moving with the current immediately. Trudeau cursed at us, and the men around him looked around like they'd woken up from a bad dream. They scattered, leaving Trudeau to wallow in his failure to stop us.

If my theory was correct, Trudeau wouldn't be able to use magic until he removed the stone from his leg. He'd also walk with a limp for the rest of his days, thanks to Della hitting her target.

"How'd you learn to shoot like that?" I asked.

"A girl's gotta know how to protect herself," Della teased and smiled up at me.

# CHAPTER 11

1820

*W*e spent two days on the river. The crew took their compensation and continued toward New Orleans, and we had to travel by foot to Fort Smith. My first course of action when we reached land was to change into my trousers. Luckily, Ric had not only gathered our belongings, but enough provisions for the three-week trip home. Considering it would take at least a week to make it to Fort Smith, and we'd added seven people to our party, our rations would get us to the trading post. Then, we'd need to restock.

Traveling with the others was uncomfortable at first. Ric and I had wanted to scout ahead in our wolf form, but we hadn't ever shifted in front of anyone but our pack. We all took turns carrying supplies, except Anson's youngest. She skipped ahead and hummed a tune.

It wasn't until our fourth day on the trail that I heard a wild animal in the distance. To ensure everyone's safety, Ric offered to shift and travel ahead. He opted to undress and make the transition in private. Then he bounded off the trail, and I walked with the others until he came back that night. We'd made camp, and I heard Ric's thoughts reach mine.

*We don't have to worry about an animal attack.*

I was tempted to shift into my wolf form, but I'd volunteered to be on the lookout while the others rested. Ric could communicate his thoughts to me, but being in my human form meant I had to speak out loud to him.

"You didn't find anything?" I whispered out into the woods behind me.

Ric stepped out from behind a tree and inspected the area. Everyone appeared to be asleep, but the last thing we needed was for one of the children to be scared of wolf-Ric. I nodded for him to come join me, and he cautiously crept around the sleeping family. He curled up next to me, radiating a welcome heat.

*I found an old friend. The fur trader we met on our way to St. Louis, Jacob Martin. He took care of the mountain lion we heard earlier.*

My eyes widened in surprise.

"Is he hauling supplies?" I asked with a lilt of optimism, and quickly covered my mouth with my hand. I didn't want to wake anyone up.

*He is, and if we get going early enough, we can catch up to him in the morning and travel together to Fort Smith. There should be room in the wagon for the children.*

The news was a relief. My body relaxed into the tree I leaned against, and my eyelids became heavy. The scent of our campfire lulled me to sleep. It wasn't until the sun peeked over the horizon, filling the sky with hues of pink and orange, that I woke up. Ric was gone, and everyone was stirring.

"Good morning," Della greeted in a sing-song voice as she secured her bedroll with a leather tie. "Ric said something about getting an early start, so we're going to eat dried meat for breakfast while we walk. You'd better get going."

Della nodded down at my bag. The contents had been strewn over the ground, but I noticed Ric's clothes missing. He must have shifted back into his human form. As I finished stuffing everything back inside, Ric stepped out from behind the tree I'd slept against, dressed. He took the bag from me and smiled. After everything we'd been through, he didn't look fazed. His blue eyes were bright, his shirt clean, and even the scruff lining his jaw looked good.

When I stretched, my joints popped and my muscles ached. Coffee would have been welcome. I could feel the bags under my eyes, and my hair was tangled. I frowned and asked Ric, "What?"

"Here, let me help you up," Ric said and reached his hand to me. He pulled me up slowly. "You look beautiful this morning."

I tilted my head to the side and furrowed my brows. He must have wanted something. Or maybe he'd done something. I decided to shrug my suspicion off and thanked him for his compliment. We needed to start moving if we wanted to reach Jake.

Ric encouraged us to push through lunch, and it wasn't long after noon that I made out Jake's wagon in the distance. He'd paused to enjoy some pickled eggs, and at the sight of our group, he gathered his reins and rode back to meet us halfway. His shotgun still looked to be his closest friend, and the liquid in his jar of hard boiled eggs sloshed over the side as he slowed his wagon.

Jake jumped down, and his spring bench squealed with delight.

"Well, I'll be," Jake exclaimed with a grin at the sight of Ric and me. "I'm as pleased as a pup with two tails to run into y'all. That nugget y'all left me was too generous."

He inspected our party with his hands on his hips. First, he took in the large family. He reach up to grab his jar and handed the eggs to Anson, encouraging them to eat. Then his eyes landed on Della. Jake straightened his shirt and squared his shoulders.

"You were the generous one," I replied, and stepped in the way of his line of sight to Della. "And we could surely use your help now. We're headed to Fort Smith for supplies."

"It is serendipitous we found each other," Jake said with a little more refinement than I'd heard him speak with before. "I'm headed to Fort Smith, and I'd be delighted if you good people would join me."

He tipped his hat in Della's direction, and I could have sworn she blushed at his gesture.

We traveled two days together before we rode into town. Della sat with Jacob at the front of his wagon most of the time, and Anson's wife and children piled into the back. Every now and then, Ric or I would excuse ourselves and shift to explore the trail ahead. We had no desire to stay at Fort Smith for long, but when we arrived, everyone else was excited to be in the hustle and bustle of town.

It was the first week of November, and it would be impossible to get through the mountains if we waited much longer. We knew the Rockies would be covered in snow by the first of December, and our journey to the falls would be physically demanding. It would be freezing. In addition to supplies, we would need blankets and skins to stay warm.

I had one gold nugget left, and the rest of our trading would have to be done with red gold. The idea of using the red gold scared me, because if Trudeau caught news of it, he'd come asking questions. We didn't have the luxury of time, so we had to make a decision about how to proceed in a day or two. Otherwise, we may not make it back to the settlement at all.

"Anson, have you considered our invitation?" Ric asked between spoonfuls of stew.

The magic-wielding cowboy nodded his head. He flattened his mustache out with a hand, covering his mouth. I couldn't tell if he was still considering it or avoiding giving us his answer. So I shoved some stew in my mouth and waited for his answer.

"Whatever you decide, it should be what you think is best for your family," Ric encouraged his new friend, and patted his back.

Anson scraped the bottom of his tin bowl with his spoon, and said, "Since you put it that way, I should shoot straight with ya and admit I have reservations. I mean, I don't want you thinking we don't appreciate everything you've done for us. But my ancestors haven't had much luck establishing towns."

The problem wasn't the Corey family or the Kasun pack, but it was supernaturals and humans trying to control each other. I couldn't argue with Anson, because he'd lost some of his loved ones in Salem, and he almost lost the rest of them in St. Louis. Trudeau would have killed them all to get what he wanted.

"If you don't go with us, you have to let us help you somehow," I reasoned, and pulled out a few of the red gold nuggets. "You'll have to be careful trading with these so Trudeau doesn't find you."

Anson started to shake his head, refusing the gift.

"You must take them," Ric encouraged sternly. "It's the only way we'll be able to move on without you in good conscience."

I leaned forward with my hand outstretched. Anson was hesitant, but he finally took them. The red gold sandwiched between our palms glowed. I pulled away, and the shining copper color dulled.

"What was that?" Della asked, sitting down next to me.

"What was what?" Jake asked from behind her. "I missed it."

"Oh, nothing," I answered. "We were just discussing plans to move on tomorrow, but Anson and his crew are thinking about sticking around here."

"Well, I'll be replenishing my inventory, since you bought everything including my wagon," Jake said, rolling his eyes teasingly, like he'd been put out by it.

The rest of us chuckled, but Jake couldn't take his eyes off Della when she smiled. He'd been doting on her since they met. Della was cautious, even shy, but I could tell she'd taken a liking to Jake, too.

Ric started talking to Jake about possible trails we could take and the weather, so I took the opportunity to check in with Della.

"Della," I called softly, trying to broach the topic gently. "I know you've always wanted to explore the continent. And you're more than welcome to travel with us to the Rockies. It's just, I was thinking, if Jake has to restock, he'll be setting out for places you've dreamed of visiting."

"That's true," she agreed bashfully, "but I'll have to join life forces with a tree soon."

"You will, but maybe instead of picking any old tree you could find the tree you were meant to be with." I winked at her and glanced at Jake, hoping she caught my meaning.

"After meeting Jake, I don't think any old tree will ever do," Della admitted and tucked a strand of hair behind her ear.

At the sound of his name or simply the sound of Della's voice, Jake perked up and gave Della his full attention. "Did you need me?" he asked.

She just smiled and nodded.

The first week of traveling through Arkansas Territory was a breeze compared to the following two weeks. The temperatures in the mountains were thirty degrees cooler, and the air was thinner. Our wagon held together as we drove through creeks and around plateaus. The horses were tired, but we were careful not to work them too hard.

The first week of December we arrived in Kasun Pack territory, and a dusting of snow covered the frozen ground. I'd expected to be ankle-deep in the powder. As we approached the settlement, the Gregs waited for us at the tree line, having been on patrol.

"Gaby, Ric," Helena called out in surprise at the sight of us. "It is so good to see you both. We weren't sure if you'd make it back."

"Why do you say that?" I asked, and grinned at Ric.

Helena shrugged and bit her bottom lip. Her mate, Boris, answered in a gruff voice, "We thought you were dead."

"Oh, well, I'm not," I said, nervous about what we could be walking into if everyone thought I'd died in St. Louis. "How have things been here?"

"Miserable," Boris answered honestly.

"Interesting," Helena said at the same time, trying to soften the blow.

Ric and I laughed. Things hadn't changed that much while we were gone. There were definitely a few pack members pushing the boundaries I'd set. And we found out the whole pack felt my absence as alpha like Ric had after I was shot. It seemed, for the past four weeks, the Novaks and Horvats had given everyone a glimpse of what their lives would be like if I weren't alpha.

So when we pulled the wagon in front of our cabin, we were welcomed by most of the pack with hugs and kind words. They were genuinely happy to see us, and the pile of supplies gave everyone hope we'd survive the winter months.

Once everyone went back to their cabins, Ric and I decided to take a walk. We'd bundled up, and as we made the trek to the falls, I appreciated everything familiar about the canyon we called home.

A cold mist stung my cheeks as we walked around the pool at the bottom of the falls. I paused to take it all in, and Ric came behind me and wrapped his arms around my shoulders. I took a deep breath, and the cold, damp air burned inside my lungs.

"You did it," Ric said, proud of me.

"No, *we* did it," I replied, and turned to face him. Ric pulled me closer, and I no longer thought of the brisk air or magical water. I only thought of him. I tilted my chin up and pressed my lips to his.

# EPILOGUE

1860

"The End," I whispered, and pressed a kiss to Conall's forehead. His blinks started growing longer after I told him Trudeau was shot. And he fell asleep around the part when Jake joined back up with us, but I couldn't not finish.

"I think I like your version better." Ric winked at me as he tucked Conall's quilt under his legs. "But since he fell asleep, you could have described that kiss in more detail."

I swatted at Ric's arm playfully, and said, "The true story is way better than that pack of lies you've been telling him."

We tiptoed out of the room, and once in the hallway, Ric turned to face me. He leaned down and wrapped his arms around me. I ran my fingers through his wavy, black hair and noticed a smudge of dirt under his ear. I tried to wipe it away, but it wouldn't budge.

"You still have dirt all over you," I said with furrowed brows, examining his neck and arms for more.

"I know a way to fix that," Ric grinned and scooped me up, startling me. He carried me through the kitchen, where pots of water were being heated on the stove. He set me down in front of the back door and asked, "It's not too late for a bath, is it?"

We hope you enjoyed this story in the Legends of Havenwood Falls series featuring a variety of supernatural creatures. The series is a collaborative effort by multiple authors.

Havenwood Falls books by Kallie Ross, following the Kasun Pack:
*Written in the Stars*
*A Pack of Lies*
*Promise the Moon*
*Defying Gravity*

Books in the historical Legends of Havenwood Falls series:

*Lost in Time* by Tish Thawer
*Dawn of the Witch Hunters* by Morgan Wylie
*Redemption's End* by Eric R. Asher
*Trapped Within a Wish* by Brynn Myers
*Blood and Damnation* by Belinda Boring
*Fated Beginnings* by E.J. Fechenda
*Emeline* by Katie M. John
*Released From a Curse* by Brynn Myers
*A Pack of Lies* by Kallie Ross
*Kiss the Ashes* by Desiree Lafawn
*Hidden Truths* by Colleen Nye
*Wrath and Retribution* by Belinda Boring
*Changing Fate* by Char Webster
*Rise of the Witch Hunters* by Morgan Wylie

*The Drowning Bride* by Seven Jane

Also try the main Havenwood Falls series; the YA line, Havenwood Falls High; the darker, sexier side of town, Havenwood Falls Sin & Silk; and the local supernatural college, Sun & Moon Academy.

Stay up to date at www.HavenwoodFalls.com

Subscribe to our reader group and receive free stories and more!

# ABOUT THE AUTHOR

*Writing unique adventures with heart.*

Kallie Ross has a passion for writing that has become an adventure in itself. She desires to create unique young adult fiction that incorporates legend, conjecture, fantasy, and conviction.

In addition to loving her life as a writer, Kallie adores being a wife, mother, friend, and teacher. She began her creative journey with books, a blog, a podcast, and lots of caffeine. Ross never imagined her own adventure would be filled with so many wonderful people or words!

KallieRoss.com

@KallieRoss {Instagram & Twitter}

Kallie Ross Books {Facebook}

# ACKNOWLEDGMENTS

Thank you, Kristie Cook, for trusting me with this *legend*. Ric Kasun is a pillar in the Havenwood Falls community and writing a small piece of his history has been a blast. I couldn't have finished this story without Gaby Robbins's friendship. She is just as inspirational as Gaby Kasun, and definitely more fierce when it comes to her family and friends. Jessica Gibson was also a huge support and encouragement.

My family is always supportive of my writing, and I am truly grateful for that blessing. Whether I'm hashing out an outline over breakfast or talking through a scene in car line, my husband and kids always speak into my storytelling.

Lastly, I want to thank the Havenwood Falls readers. Your enthusiasm for this world keeps me dreaming up stories and writing them down. Thank you!

# AN EXCERPT

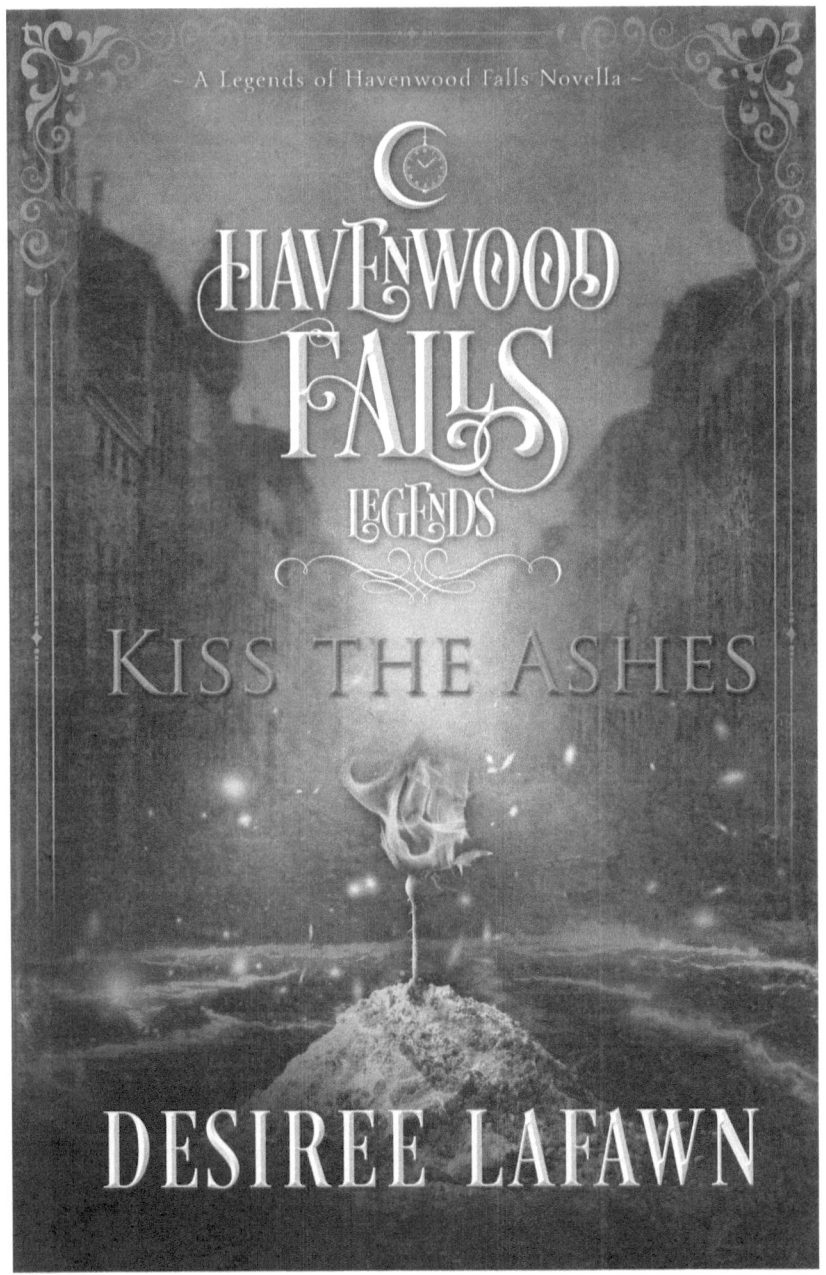

~ A Legends of Havenwood Falls Novella ~

# HAVENWOOD FALLS LEGENDS

## KISS THE ASHES

## DESIREE LAFAWN

## *Kiss the Ashes* (A Legends of Havenwood Falls Novella) by Desiree Lafawn

Mocked, ridiculed, and sentenced to death, seven-year-old River is saved from the noose when the Sisters McNee find her. They take her to their home in Havenwood Falls, a place for people like her to live safely, without fear of persecution. But what if the threat to their safety is River herself?

Her fire-maiden origins are a mystery. One a child has no hope of explaining. Then one futuristic vision from a well-respected member of the community seals her fate.

Flames.

Chaos.

Complete destruction.

Sixteen years later, River has come of age in the era of prosperity, prohibition, and ragtime music—and even as an adult, she still hates her power, resolute to never use it again. She tries to stay under the radar, but there is no hiding from the penetrating eyes of Jonas Pederson. Despite repeated warnings that she is dangerous, he won't stop pursuing her until she understands that he can easily survive her flames—even if he needs to show her his own well-protected secret.

It might be too late for River, though, when a threat from the past ignites that horrible vision.

Flames.

Chaos.

Destruction.

In the end, it will all be ashes.

# KISS THE ASHES

I would never get used to hard-soled shoes even as an adult, but as a girl of seven I hated them. I'd much rather have gone barefoot, but the teachers in Carlisle were adamant the children properly dress themselves at all times. Dressed according to their standards, anyway. Our parents stood opposed even as the soldiers dragged us from the reservation.

"Who are you to take our children?" they cried out, unable to do more than shake their fists and stomp their feet; our once proud nation reduced to servants of a government foreign to us. A government so hell-bent on erasing our existence they uprooted the native children and forced them into boarding schools to learn the English way. Eliminate the savages and teach the children to be productive members of society.

*Kill the Indian. Save the man.*

Even now, many years later and grown, I have trouble wrapping my mind around the thought process that led to the exodus of the children—the reeducation process. But that had happened. And the history books will more than likely gloss it over the more time marches on, but I will never forget being five years old and plucked from the small plot of land I considered my home.

Parents wept.

But not my parents. They died of the great sickness a year before. I had no parents to hold me in their arms as the soldiers came and separated us. No one fought for me, so when the time came to leave—aside from dragging my heels in the dirt—nothing stopped the soldiers from putting me on the wagon, squeezing me up against the rows of other crying, terrified children.

But I was different. If they knew how different, would they have placed me with the other children? Would they have taken me? There was no way to know, and I wouldn't explain because I had learned long ago that *my* kind of different was best kept hidden. Even from my own people.

So to the Carlisle Indian Industrial School I went, sandwiched in with many other children from mixed tribes, all learning to speak English and change everything about themselves. The administration beat the students who cried, and the angry, rebellious ones received a harsher punishment. One so severe, we feared talking about it amongst ourselves—because those students left without warning and didn't come back. But I didn't cry, and I didn't rebel. I obeyed, because I knew no other way. And there I lived for two years, suffering at the hands of my oppressors under the guise of spiritual cleansing until the summer of my seventh year.

I made a mistake.

It was playtime in the yard. That short time of day between morning chores and evening chores when there was a small sliver of space to remember that we were just children. It was my favorite time, and every chance I thought I could get away with it, I'd chuck my shoes under the shade of a white oak tree and curl my toes in the grass. Not running, not moving, just standing in place, anchored to the earth. Eyes closed, I stood under the tree with my arms raised out to the sides, feeling the wind above and below me.

*The Great Thunder is near*, I thought to myself, smelling the rain on the wind. *I wonder what mischief the Thunder Boys will be up to tonight.* The Great Thunder and his sons were a myth, and I dared not speak of it out loud, not when the teachers could hear. Speaking the stories of my people was forbidden and the punishment severe. But since no one controlled what went on in my head, I would think as I pleased.

"Come back here, Thomas," a voice shouted angrily, interrupting my peaceful moment. "You've stolen the bread; we know you have. Come receive your punishment."

A small brown blur came running across the packed dirt yard, and children of various ages stopped mid-play to see the boy running with the bit of bread locked in his fist. He came to a screeching halt about fifteen feet from where I stood, under my oak tree, and facing off like a boxer, he scowled at his aggressor.

I recognized the boy from my old village. I remembered when his mother had clung to him and the soldiers yanked him, only a year younger than myself, from her grieving arms. They'd given him a new name when he'd come to this school, just as they'd done me, but I knew his real name was Wesa. I knew because his mother had screamed it to the sky as they had taken away the children.

Wesa. Two years he'd been here, knowing the rules. And still he stole the bread.

*Oh, Wesa, what will happen to you now?*

Thomas now, no longer Wesa, stood in front of the man who'd been so aggressively calling his name. His cotton button-down shirt had come untucked from his plain brown breeches while chasing the boy, and he stood, panting, mouth drawn down in a formidable frown.

"Thomas. You've stolen food. Accept the punishment." The man's expression was stern, his eyes hard and unfeeling.

Wesa fidgeted before opening his hand to show the small bit of bread clutched in his fist. "But I'm so hungry, Mr. Crane." He looked at the food, his eyes wet and his lower lip trembling. "Please, I didn't want to steal, but I'm so hungry."

Sorrow gripped my heart for him. My stomach often felt hollow from the slim allotment of rations we were each given per day. And he was so young. *Poor Wesa*. Mr. Crane's features relaxed, and I breathed an inaudible sigh of relief. Mr. Crane was not a very nice man by nature, but I'd never *seen* him hurt any of the students. The same couldn't be said for other teachers. Several of them seemed to only be working at the boarding school because they loved tormenting children, seeking reasons to dole out discipline.

Mr. Crane just always had a sour look on his face, and even though he always smelled like whiskey, I'd never seen him raise his hand in anger.

"Bring it, Thomas." Mr. Crane raised his hand and beckoned Thomas closer. Two tears snaked down the small boy's cheeks, but the will of the older man won, and the younger of the two made slow shuffling steps across the packed dirt of the yard, head hanging low in defeat. Eyes so downcast he didn't see the blow coming and didn't even get to react. My seven-year-old self could do nothing but watch openmouthed at the violence that unfolded.

The cuff on the side of his six-year-old head lifted him straight off the ground and onto his back where he lay, a sad pile of arms and legs in the dirt.

"Thieves are beaten, Thomas," Mr. Crane said calmly, standing over the small boy on the ground too stunned to even react as the older man plucked the bread from his now slack grip. He grimaced and crumbled the small loaf with one hand until it was nothing but crumbs drifting to the ground. I mourned the loss of the food myself, hand drifting to my empty stomach. Now no one would get to eat it.

"If we let you do it, then everyone would think it entitled them to more than we give them, boy. You aren't special. None of you are. But if you're so hungry, you can eat your bread in the mud like an animal. Are you an animal, Thomas?" Mr. Crane's face twisted into something monstrous, and he stepped on the small pile of bread crumbs with his dusty brown shoe. "Go on, Thomas; eat it if you're hungry. This is good enough for you."

The small boy looked up from his place on the ground, afraid to move. More tears fell down his face, his little shoulders shaking with fear—or pain—maybe both. He made no move toward the pile in the dirt and crumbs, and still I stood in place, caught inside the vision with no way out. Mr. Crane sneered at him, his eyes a window to the depths of an ugly soul. Without warning, Mr. Crane's leg shot out, and his dirty brown shoe connected with the small boy's legs, lifting him up a few inches and sending him spinning farther in the dirt. Wesa—or Thomas, as they called him —lay on his back, clutching his side and crying. He made no move to get to his feet.

The air no longer smelled of rain. Instead, the wind carried the scent of burning. Similar to that of the blaze we gathered around when we had our own land, where the warriors told the tales of the hunt and the women sang their songs and cooked the meat. It was the smell of the fatwood just sparking, smoky and warm but not yet blistering. It was a small fire, but with enough tending it would become a great blaze, hot enough to sear anything placed before it. The breeze tickled my skin and moved the stray hairs that stuck out of my braids around my face. I didn't know where the wind had come from, but it did nothing to cool the aching itch marching up and down my skin, nor the anger that was bubbling just below the surface.

Mr. Crane was hurting Wesa—and no one was doing a thing to stop it.

He was a small boy, not so different from myself, who was just hungry. We all were, and that was a fact, but he was only six and didn't have as much of a grasp of self-control, even after two years in their Anglo prison. But Mr. Crane would make an example out of him regardless. The older man bore down on the child, his face as red as his facial hair, a grim smile plastered on his face.

*He's happy.* My inner thoughts echoed the stark reality. Even as a young child, I still understood. *He wants to hurt Wesa.*

But Wesa was so small, he couldn't take much more. Still no one in the yard moved. All those small faces looked on with fear in their eyes. No one would stand up for Wesa; no one could. Everyone knew what the punishment for rebellion was. I had seen the stone markings before—set up in the woods a short bit away from the school. That's where rebellion led you—to your very own stone marking in the dirt.

But even so, watching Mr. Crane as he reached the spot where he had kicked the young boy and hauled him back to his feet by his close-cropped hair had me gritting my teeth, the taste of bile and ash in my throat. He cocked back his fist and hit Wesa once; the impact split the skin on his chin and blood spurted out. Wesa cried. The smoke in the air stung my eyes, and my voice was that of a stranger croaking out of a throat lined with rocks and silt.

"No."

I wasn't loud enough. Mr. Crane didn't hear me, or at least pretended he didn't as he shook the boy until his feet left the ground, and he hung there in his master's hands, limp as an animal removed from a trap. "Come, Thomas, to punishment with you."

*To punishment.* As if the six-year-old hadn't been through enough. There was nowhere that Mr. Crane would take him that could be any improvement, and I doubted Wesa could even walk by himself. Blood poured from that angry cut on his face, and the crimson trail dripping from his tiny chin matched the hue of my blistering rage.

I found my voice.

"No." The heated breeze carried the word farther this time. This time Mr. Crane heard me, and his head snapped up, his eyes zeroing in on me from where he stood a short distance away. His mouth dropped open, but he didn't release his hold on the small boy.

"Mary, what are you doing?" *Mary.* That was my new name. I wasn't supposed to think of myself as River anymore, but sometimes I forgot. Times like now, when the atrocity I had just witnessed placed me somewhere outside of myself—outside of my safety nets and away from right and wrong.

I was just so *angry.*

Uncertainty graced Mr. Crane's face, and he took a small step back. I didn't want him to take a step back. I wanted him to let go of Wesa.

"No. You let him go. You hurt him—you're a bad man." The air snapped and crackled around me, and my braids rose and fell in this new heated breeze before unraveling completely. My long tresses danced in the angry wind.

"What are you doing?" the older man whispered, his eyes no longer narrow and cruel, but wide and fearful. "What are you—? Stay back. Stay away—"

But I didn't stay away. I couldn't, because Mr. Crane still had his meaty hand fisted in Wesa's short dark hair and was dragging him backward across the ground. Rage burned in my belly. He was a bad man. He hurt Wesa. He needed to be punished.

The ground I stood on cracked beneath my feet, the air so hot, the dirt released what little moisture it had and hardened like wood. The small bit of grass I'd curled my toes in earlier incinerated as if it had never been. I barely noticed. The heat. The smell. The acidic swell burning and churning deep in my belly—all were secondary to my rage as I looked at the man who had beaten a small boy to near unconsciousness.

"Drop him." The words blasted out of my mouth with ferocity, and Mr. Crane complied without thinking. Wesa just lay there, crumpled where he fell. The only movement in the entire yard was the myriad of small heads swiveling to look from Mr. Crane to me. The same look of horror that had been focused on Mr. Crane now moved to me. I didn't care.

I couldn't see any of them anymore. All I could see was the form of the man in front of me, the one who had such blackness in his soul, he could beat a child with a smile on his face. I only had eyes for him. Two other teachers had come into the yard by now— Mr. Weisman and Mrs. Crane. They had come out to see what was going on, I was sure, but I couldn't count on either of them to help in this situation. No, I'd witnessed their punishments before. No help would come from any of the adults in this building. I'd need to take care of them myself.

"What on earth is going on out here? Oh—" Mrs. Crane's sentence ended in a bloodcurdling shriek. "Mary! It's witchcraft! Savage witchcraft!"

I ignored her. I was far too focused on the backward steps of Mr. Crane as he tried to put as much space between the two of us as possible. Mr. Weisman had no such sense of self-preservation, and he marched to where I stood, circumventing Wesa on the ground as if he was nothing more than a puddle of dirty water. He almost made it in time to stop me. Almost.

I felt the graze of his fingers on my arm before I opened my mouth to scream. Dry, cracked lips pulled back as far as I was able, but no sound escaped. I spoke no words because I had none to give. But I had something else. That which I had been hiding for as long as I could remember. That twisting ache in my guts I had spent years learning to ignore, or at least keep hidden from everyone around me. My parents had taught me that, if not much else. Hide it away or bad things would happen.

Well, I'd hidden it all this time, and bad things still happened. There was no need to hide it anymore, so I let the mangled ropes of burning fury snake their way out of the depths of my body and erupt from my mouth in a single blast of heat and flame. I might not have any words to exorcise my rage, but I did have my fire.

~

As a child I'd never thought of killing anyone before. I'd seen dead people, but I'd never inflicted damage on another human soul intending to end their life. But with Mr. Crane lying in a pile on the charred ground in front of me, I was having trouble dredging up any regret about what I had done.

Especially when I could still see the little ball of crying boy on the ground just a little farther away.

Mr. Crane was a bad man.

He also wasn't dead. The fire had spewed forth from my belly angry and hot, but it had done little damage besides heating the air and charring his hair and clothes. He threw himself on the ground in what was probably a mixture of self-preservation and fear, and had smothered the flames most likely without even thinking about it.

I'd acted without thinking, as most children do, but my actions still had the desired effect. Mr. Crane had stopped hurting Wesa. I'd not thought a single second past that goal, and I wasn't prepared to defend myself as the hands of the other adults in the yard descended on my seven-year-old self, slinging me over a meaty shoulder by my legs as my hair hung down over my face, obscuring my vision.

"Get her out of here, Hank," Mrs. Crane squawked as Mr. Weisman carted me out of the yard at a run. "I don't know what dirty little trick she pulled, but she won't get another chance. Lock her away until we decide on her punishment. Get up, Yancy," she leveled at Mr. Crane where he still lay on the ground. "You've been had by the tricks of a child. You're an embarrassment to everyone."

She may have had more to say, but Mr. Weisman carried me too far to hear, and I couldn't see through the hair that hung down over my face. He carried me far enough that the blood rushing to my head obliterated any sound at all, and I had trouble getting my bearings as I was suddenly righted and sat down on an upside-down crate in a dark room I'd never been in before.

With my hair now out of my face and the blood that had been thundering in my head receding, I could see the face of Mr. Weisman as he towered above me.

"I'm afraid you've stepped in something you can't step out of, Mary girl." He sighed and scrubbed his hands over his face. I didn't want to think about what he meant, but I couldn't help but notice I was in an old storeroom out back, away from other people, and not back in the dormitory to await a normal punishment like I had thought I would be. "I know you thought you were helping Thomas, but it will only be worse for you now, you know? Not sure what they'll do with you, but it can't be good from the look of things. You attacked a teacher. They'll nip that right away, I'm sure."

I said nothing, just looked up at Mr. Weisman, trying not to let the fear I felt show on my face. I'd learned long ago to hide the things that were strange about me. To swallow it down and not let it out. It wasn't just strangers and those at the school who would persecute me if they knew. My own people were not immune to fear either. My parents had taught me long ago that the world was a dangerous place, and I knew the cost of letting my power show.

But my parents died, and I'd revealed my secret.

Not a single soul in this world would help me now.

"Hold out your hands, then, Mary," Mr. Weisman said as he pulled a heavy cord from a hook on the wall. Willing my arms not to shake, I did as he asked. "Now Michelle thinks you pulled some trick on Yancy to get him to leave Thomas alone, but I was there. I know what I saw. Even now I see—your eyes are straight black, all the way through. Just a little bit of the white showing on the outside now, when there was none earlier. That's not normal, girl."

He continued to speak as he wound the corded rope around my wrists, binding my hands together in front of me. I didn't know what to say to him. I'd only used my fire once before, and only in front of my parents, so I didn't know my eyes changed colors at all.

"I know you're something different. I've met others like you before. Well, not exactly like you. I don't know what you are," he said as he cut off the trailing ends of rope and patted my knee where I sat. "Once met a man who could tell things would happen before they did. Knew a lady that could tell what you were thinking when the words hadn't even left your mouth yet. You're someone like them, I suppose, although that was a pitiful display back there." Stepping away from me and walking toward the door, he paused, his back to me. "I hope it was worth it, Mary. You might have gotten the eyes off young Thomas, but now they're all on you. Lord knows what they're going to do with you now. That Michelle—she doesn't have a compassionate bone in her body. It's a damn shame, it is, but you called her attention on you now."

So he was one of *those* kind, then. I'd met people like Hank Weisman before. People who didn't like the hard-hearted things they saw going on around them, but did nothing to fix them. It wasn't that he wanted to tie me up—he didn't want anything bad to happen to me. He just didn't care enough to help me, even though he knew it would be bad. I hoped that when I died, as I was going to, I could come back to the earth in another time period, when the world wasn't full of so many evil people and cowards.

If everyone was just a little bit braver, we could change the world.

Taking my silence as acceptance, Mr. Weisman opened the door to leave, letting a tiny sliver of sunlight in through the open door, illuminating the rest of the room I was being held in. It was a storage room—mostly extra wood and tools—as well as drums of oil for lamps stacked in a corner.

"You'll need to sit tight for a while, Miss Mary, until she comes for you. I wouldn't try any of your fancy smoke effects either—I doubt even you would survive the explosion if you breathe hot in here." And with that, he shut me in, locking the door behind him and eliminating the only light in the entire room.

I didn't know if I would survive or not. I didn't know a single thing about my power to produce fire besides the fact that I could do it at all. It wasn't something that had passed from my parents, that was for sure. No one knew what I was, or what I was capable of; we only knew to suppress it so no one would find out. And this was why. I may have saved Wesa temporarily, but I had doomed myself instead. It terrified my seven-year-old self, and I cried in the dark, knowing there would be no one to let me out even if I made enough noise to be heard.

After an undetermined amount of time sitting on the edge of the crate with my bound hands in my lap, my back cramping and complaining, I slid to the floor and rested my back against the wood. I must have rested my eyes as well, because they popped open with a start when the storage room door opened. No daylight streamed in through the doorway this time, so I guessed they had confined me for half a day at least, as it was full night. The soft light of an oil lantern flickered in the doorway for an instant, and then I saw nothing but blackness as a heavy sack was pulled tight over my head and they lifted me to my feet.

I thought I'd been afraid when the soldiers had come and rounded up the children to go to that school in the first place. I knew nothing then. Crying in the solitude of the darkened storage shed, with my hands bound in front of me and my legs shaking with dread, I'd been woefully unprepared. For no other experience in my life compared to the absolute terror of having my eyes covered and my body slung over the shoulder of a man who wasn't Mr. Weisman this time.

The smell of whiskey filled my nose, and it wasn't until they dumped me into the back of a wagon and the horse moved that I understood who had taken me.

"You're drunk, Yancy. Can you even see to steer the horse? Move aside. Give me the reins." That was the voice of Mrs. Crane for sure. I didn't know where we were going, but I could tell by the way my little body bumped and rolled around in the cart it was uneven ground, and by the length of time we traveled, I imagined we were quite a way from the school.

It's a terrifying thing for any adult—that moment of realization when they know *without a shred of doubt* they are living their last moments. But for me, as a child who'd only known the fear of hiding my entire life, it was a different feeling. The rough fibers of fraying rope digging into the sensitive skin over my collarbone and the dark canvas bag that had been slapped over my head just seemed like the obvious ending to my short, pitiful story.

This wasn't punishment. This was death. I deserved this end, and I didn't belong here.

They never took the bag off my head, not even for a moment. Not when they slid me feet first off the wagon and made me walk behind them, my hands still bound in front of me and someone, probably Mr. Crane, leading by the rope already tied around my neck. I stumbled once, and the rope pulled tight, cutting my airway closed. Was this what it would be like to die? I didn't want it. Panic bloomed in my chest, and I cried, my sobs fighting to be free from my already restricted throat.

"It's too late for that, you little witch," Mrs. Crane hissed in my ear. "Every opportunity we've given you to become a good Christian, and you resort to filthy heathen ways."

"Attacked me, she did," Mr. Crane hiccupped from somewhere

in front of me. "Burned the whiskers right off my chin. Can't let that go. One bad apple, you know, Michelle?"

"Yes, Yancy, I know. You have to cull the herd to keep the sheep in line. We won't suffer troublemakers, Mary."

I wanted to yell and scream. I wanted to tell them my name wasn't Mary, but I couldn't say a word. That rope cutting the air from my lungs, even just briefly, froze my entire body. Any amount of energy I had left was focusing on moving one foot in front of the other in a straight line, so I didn't stumble again.

Then we stopped walking, and no one spoke again for quite some time. The silence was just as unnerving as when they were talking. There were the light sounds of people at work, like the Cranes were setting up whatever they would do, and I was left to stand by a tree with my hands still tied in front of me and the rough bark scraping against my back. It was difficult to breathe inside the sack on my head, but after that tiny taste of suffocation, any breaths were a luxury.

I thought I'd imagined it—a shuffling behind the tree I was standing against, a quiet whispering through the tall grass that tickled my shins. But it continued, and as I strained my ears to catch the sounds that the Cranes were too busy to notice, a small voice carried through the air next to my head, as if coming from my mind itself.

"Little girl," it whispered. "Don't make a sound, but if you can hear me, tap your foot two times." I was sure I was crazy. A disembodied voice in the woods. Talking to me. And only I could hear it? Maybe I was going insane before they put me to death. I was too young to know any better.

"Sister, you have to be more specific. Maybe she doesn't understand what you mean?" A different yet similar voice to the first floated by my other ear.

"Will you be quiet and let me work? I'm trying not to scare her, and you're jabbering away."

"Sister, just tell her we'll help her. If she knows, she'll be able to handle the after parts."

"You're right, sister," the first voice replied. "We will help you, dear. If you understand that, can you tap your left foot two times? It doesn't have to be a big tap; we'll be able to see it."

I tapped my left foot two times softly in the grass. I could hear the Cranes moving around in the near distance, somehow missing the entire exchange. I did not understand what was going on, but the strange voices whispering were the friendliest I'd heard in ages, so I listened.

"Okay now, dear, just do what they want you to do and don't be afraid anymore. It will get loud . . ."

"It's going to sound like the hounds of hell are coming for their souls, if we play our cards right," the other voice interrupted, still barely a thought on the breeze, "but it should get their britches in a twist enough for us to steal you away."

"Yes, thank you, sister," the first voice chided. "We'll be stealing you away, is that all right?" For what purpose they would be stealing me for I didn't know, but it couldn't be as bad as dying at the end of a dirty rope, so I nodded my head slightly, and the voice continued. "It will be loud, dear, and I'm sorry ahead of time for that, but you can't move, okay? Act like you don't hear it at all."

And then the voices disappeared, and I felt the slack on the rope tighten as the Cranes finished whatever prep work had kept them busy for the last few minutes. I wasn't sure what would happen, but hope swelled in my small chest as I gave myself over to the possibility I might just get saved.

www.ingramcontent.com/pod-product-compliance
Lightning Source LLC
Chambersburg PA
CBHW051959170626
46808CB00007B/2699